Monster

Curse of the Hybrids

Book 6

LISA LAGALY

PUBLISHING

Published in the United States of America

First Printing, 2025

ISBN
ebook: 978-1-966455-14-1
print: 978-1-966455-15-8

LL Publishing
Lisa1.author@gmail.com

Previously

Between 1346 and 1353, a horrible pestilence, later known as the Black Death, swept across Europe, killing perhaps 50% of the population. A seer, whose name is now lost to history, blamed the intermingling of witches and wolves and foresaw that the only way to stop the pestilence was to destroy those with mixed blood and prevent their existence. Desperate for a cure, four powerful witches helped him craft a curse to ensure hybrids and those who protected them were eradicated. To make certain the curse would last, they copied it onto five tablets and spread them around the globe. Several hundred years later, four tablets are thought to still exist.

After Brayton was nearly killed by a fire witch, Brayton's dad announced Honey's existence to the world. Realizing her only hope of a normal life was to find and destroy the hybrid curse, she began searching for the four remaining tablets. She found a clue while hiding out in Rome and eventually found a tablet, but recovering it led to the death of her traveling companion and friend. To protect her from blame for his death, his ghost marked Honey as his Luna. Six days later, under the full moon, she was given a choice to choose another alpha: either a stranger or Brayton. She chose Brayton. Now she has three stars across her forehead, can speak telepathically, and apparently has a fated mate, or so Brayton claims.

1

HONEY - NOVEMBER 15 - AUSTRALIA

"I'll see you at Christmas break, if not sooner," Brayton said, kissing the tip of her nose.

Honey resisted the urge to back away, not because she didn't like it, but because it was weird. She'd never kissed anyone on the nose or the lips before, although if all kisses were like the one Brayton had planted on her under the full moon, she now understood why people liked to kiss. Were they all like that or was it just ones you got at a Luna induction ceremony by your possible fated mate? She kinda wanted to try again.

Nathan released a loud sigh. "Come on, Lover Boy, I calculate it's already 7 am back home. We need to get back to the dorms and take showers and eat breakfast."

"I think it's only 6 am," Walter said.

"Either way, we need to be going."

Brayton clasped both of Honey's hands in his. "You could come with us."

She wanted to, badly but, "I could, but then I'd have to hide in a basement or your cars or something and you'd have to supply me with food and you'd get caught. That won't work."

He huffed out a sad-sounding sigh, "I know."

"And you can't just abandon your family and pack at Christmas. Your mom would be devastated," and she really didn't want Luna Lynn to have another reason to hate her.

"But she's being so…she's impossible. I don't know how Dad stands it. She's organized around-the-clock volunteers to take calls from anyone who thinks they've seen you."

Honey's heart tore a little. Brayton's mom had been so supportive last year, almost like her own mom.

"Does anyone ever call in?"

"All the time. None of them are real sightings though."

"That's good."

She tried to sound upbeat but must have failed because Brayton pulled her into a hug. "Hey. There's nothing you or I can do about it. Mom's stubborn and might hold a grudge against you the rest of her life, but if we can break the curse, she'll have no legal reason to pursue you anymore."

Luca shook his head. "That was the worst pep talk I've ever heard." He grabbed Honey's hand and pulled her into his arms. "Honey, you are nailing this cursed-but-not-cursed thing. Just three more pieces to go. Once you figure out where they are, we'll help you find them. I bet Blaze and the rest of our friends will too. You can stay hidden while we do the dirty work."

"That's a good plan," Walter said, tapping his index fingers on his lips the way he did when he was mulling something over. "Brayton can be the contact point. If you can get us targets by Christmas break, we can divide, retrieve, and maybe portal them to you, then you can break them all at once. Too bad portals are getting harder to come by."

"You guys keep the ones Alpha Silver sent," Honey

5

decided, pulling herself out of Luca's arms. "I've discovered another way."

"Another way?" Nathan asked.

"Yes." She reached up and tapped the top of Walter's forehead with her right pinkie, then tapped Nathan's forehead with her left pinkie, then tapped Luca's forehead with her nose. "You are my anchors. If I'm ever in trouble, I'll try to get to one of you."

"What about me?" Brayton asked.

She wanted to kiss him again, just because, and he certainly seemed to like kissing her but it felt weird to ask him for hugs, let alone a kiss. He had to be wrong about the fated mate thing. It would be a good place to set her anchor though.

"Um, kiss me."

"You're going to anchor yourself to my lips?"

"Mmm-hmm."

"With your lips?"

She felt herself turning red again. "I have to touch each of you with a unique part of my body that I don't use to anchor to anything else so I know who I'm going to. I don't plan on kissing anyone else so…"

He cut her off with another kiss so outstanding, she nearly forgot to plant her anchor. It didn't help her oddly weak knees at all when he whispered "That is the sexiest thing anyone has ever said or did to me. You can anchor yourself to my lips any time."

"That gives a whole new meaning to lip-locked," Luca commented.

"Just stop," Nathan said.

"Do you have to touch a body? Could it be a thing?" Walter asked.

"It can be a thing," Honey said, latching onto Walter's lifeline and backing out of Brayton's arms, "but if I gave you a rock and then you buried it in a drawer or dropped it in the water or even lost it under your bed, I'm not sure what would happen when I followed the link. If I touch your heads, you should at least be where there's air and hopefully room."

"Does that mean you could pop to us anywhere, even in the shower?" Luca asked.

"Yes, but you don't spend much time in the shower, so that won't be a problem for you," she teased.

"I do spend a lot of time in the bathroom though, especially after tacos. Taco Tuesday. Remember that."

She nodded sincerely. "Believe me, I will."

"Pop to me first," Brayton whispered in her ear. His breath sent shivers down her spine. "I will always be ready for you."

"That's a good line. No wonder alphas are so popular,' Luca said.

"Can we go already," Nathan whined. "I can't be late to my class again."

"Yes," Walter said, pulling Honey into his arms for one of his excellent hugs. "Brayton, I could open the portal to my car. I parked it where I doubt anyone would notice us popping out."

"No. It's infested with spy spells again. I'll send us back to the bathroom."

"What if someone is using it," Luca asked. "Plus, is Walmart even open right now?"

"What about my dorm room. No one should be there," Nathan said.

"But then our cars would still be at Walmart. Brayton,

why not the inside of your SUV," Walter suggested.

"I can't see us stepping into it, but we could step out of the passenger door and into the parking lot."

"Yes, that will work," Walter agreed.

"Goodbye, Honey," Nathan said, pulling her into his own hug and planting a kiss on her cheek. "Congratulations on your Lunaness. And thanks for helping me win the bet."

"You didn't win. You bet it would be Christmas!" Luca protested.

"I'm the closest."

"Close only works with horseshoes and hand-grenades," Walter droned.

"What bet?" Honey asked.

"How long it would take for you two to get together," Walter said.

Honey scrunched her nose at them. "Why would you think we'd ever get together?"

The three of them looked at each other and burst into laughter.

"Guys, stop. Walter!" Honey slugged his shoulder.

Walter chuckled a few more times, then explained, "Brayton has been crushing on you since at least last Christmas, but you were oblivious. It was brilliant."

"I'm glad I could amuse you," she huffed, turning so she wouldn't have to look at them. Could they see her face turning red in the dark? She hoped not.

"Hey," Walter said, putting his arm around her. "We weren't laughing at you, we were laughing at the situation. We love you just the way you are."

"Even with my short hair?" They hadn't really said much about it. She liked it, but she couldn't help

8

wondering what her friends thought.

He rubbed his knuckles vigorously over the top of her head. "Especially with your short hair, but I like it long too."

She hugged Walter back. "You guys are the best."

"Come on!" Nathan said. "We've wasted another fifteen minutes."

"Will you be okay here tonight?" Brayton asked, looking through the trees at the free campground they'd hiked back to after their adventure under the moon.

It *was* rather thickly populated with tents, but maybe that was normal for this time of year in Australia.

"Yeah, I'm sure there's an open spot somewhere and most people are already asleep. They won't even notice me."

He grabbed her hand and pulled her to face him then lowered his head to kiss her again, long and slow and toe-curling. When he finally finished the kiss, he gave a tiny sigh, pulled her against his warm body, and leaned his head against the top of hers. She couldn't have stopped herself from melting against him if she wanted to.

"Write to me in the morning so I know you're okay."

She nodded. Now that she thought about it, he had been acting strange for a while. Being his (gulp) Luna was going to take some getting used to.

2

HONEY – NOVEMBER 18 – SYDNEY

Incense overpowered the mishmash of magic spells in the magic shop Honey had found hidden in plain sight between a colorful boutique and a hidden treasures shop, but just barely. The woman at the register, an older lady this time, was busy helping someone. Honey started slowly browsing her way back to the map section. The woman had charms for nearly everything – warts, love, hair color, protection – but, Honey checked out the competition with both her nose and her eyes, her competitor's charms weren't automatic.

"Can I help you?" a woman said right behind her.

Honey had caught the swish of the woman's skirt when she neared so she didn't jump. Pulling up a smile, Honey turned and said in her best Scottish accent, "Aye, I'd like a quaerere map."

The woman scanned Honey from her floppy hat and blond wig down to her flowy skirt and sandals. "I carry the finest maps in Sydney. Each one is designed to work for years without maintenance or recharging. You treat them right and your children's children will be able to use them."

"Barry!" Honey was pretty sure that meant good or excellent.

"Is there a certain locale you want or do you want a world set?"

"Ah would like a world map for noo."

"Then you plan to buy the more specific maps later."

Honey nodded.

"Let me show you what I have."

The map room reminded Honey of a library with the rich wood shelves covering three walls and the large wooden table in the middle. Maps of all kinds, from the folded ones you could pick up at gas stations, to scrolls in long tubes, to thick books of maps, were on the shelves.

The woman pulled a red tube from a bin in the middle of the shelf and unrolled its contents on the table. "This is my most popular model. As you can see, it's printed on quality paper, the font and markings are clear and concise, and it's protected from water and damage by a non-yellowing clear coating."

"It is very nice. Hoo much." She nearly forgot her accent. Stupid. It would have been safer not to use it at all.

"Five-thousand."

Maybe that's why there were no price tags. If you had to ask, it was going to be too much.

"How much is yer cheapest one?"

"Five-hundred, but it's much smaller and won't last nearly as long."

"Ye charge twenty for protection charms."

"They are easy to make and wear out. The magic in the maps never wears out."

"Accounting for mark up, thirty protection charms equal yer cheap map, aye?"

"Are you proposing a trade?"

Honey nodded.

The woman shook her head. "I never trade for maps. They are my bread-and-butter. I need cash to pay the bills."

Honey nodded. It had been a gamble, making the charms without asking about a trade first, but the woman, who must be the owner, hadn't been in the store when Honey visited before. Besides, she still had a marketable product with a low overhead since she'd used hairbands as the shields.

"Is thaur a market whaur ah can sell mah charms?"

"There is, but you have to be licensed and a one-time spot cost $50. A season is $500."

"How do ah get a license?"

"That costs money too. Why don't you just go to the library and use the maps there? They only charge ten dollars."

Honey prayed the woman didn't pay any attention to the news or make any connections while she started spilling her made-up story.

"Ah have a very old heirloom piece. I'm lookin' fur other pieces from th' set. Th' piece ah hav' is cursed though. Ah didnae think they'd want somethin' cursed in th' library."

"What's the curse?"

"Ah dunnae ken. Ah havenae touched it." Both true-ish. She knew what one of the curses did, but the second, the one that she was sure Mr. No-Name had put over the first, felt and smelled worse than death. Every time she pulled it out of the nether to examine it, it smelled worse. She had put the lid back on the box the last time so the curse didn't contaminate the nether.

"Then how do you know it's cursed?"

Honey gave an involuntary shiver. "It feels bad."

"They why would you search for the rest?"

12

Good question.

"Family."

It wasn't the best answer, but it was the most truthful one she could come up with if she considered all hybrids to be her family, or pack. Unfortunately, that still made her a pack of one.

"I don't understand."

Honey took a breath and regurgitated her more detailed fake story. "Many years ago some of mah family went tae th' new world and maybe here. They each took a piece of th' set. Ah am tryin' tae find mah long-lost relatives."

"Then why is it cursed?"

Honey shrugged. "Were all yer ancestors nice?"

The woman snorted.

The bell above the shop door rang and a man wearing a top hat and a cardigan walked in. From the chin up, he wouldn't have been out of place two-hundred years ago, especially with the shiny, curled mustache, but the white cardigan with the little pink flowers made him think of her grandmother. All he needed was a skirt like she was wearing. Honey realized she was staring and made herself turn back to the woman. "Thanks for yer help."

"Sorry I couldn't make the trade."

"That's all right. Ye've given me an idea."

It wasn't her favorite idea, but it had to be done.

She'd been avoiding dealing with the additional curse Mr. No-Name had placed on the curse tablet because it smelled and felt about ten times worse than the thing the kidnapper had stuck on her head last spring. The kidnapper's device had made her relive the death of her parents over and over. She'd been so lost in her mind she'd been completely unaware of what was going on around her. If she got stuck in Mr. No-Name's curse, she suspected she would most certainly die a tortured, painful death.

On the other hand, she wasn't the same girl she had been six months ago. Not only did she now have several books worth of magic lessons, she also had fifty protection charms. She could break it, she told herself, as long as it didn't take over her mind. The only other thing she needed was a place to fight the curse without interruption.

It took her a couple of days, but she found the perfect abandoned house. It was on the edge of a middle-class neighborhood bordered by a tree-lined creek. The yard was overgrown, one window was boarded up, and there was no pile of mail, suggesting the mail service had been canceled. To be certain it was empty, she transformed into her still-glowing wolf form during the day, so it wouldn't be as noticeable, and jogged into the yard like a stray dog to search for recent scents. There were none. She didn't sense any wolves or magic in the neighborhood either. Even more enticing, the back door was hidden from the neighbors and only had a single lock. She reached up with her paw and made the lock disappear.

The door stuck. She had to put her paw in the hole where the lock had been and give it several hard tugs before it opened. Stale, dry air was the only thing that greeted her. After looking around to make sure no one was watching, she popped the lock back in place, stepped through the doorway, transformed, and pulled the door shut behind her.

To her surprise, the house wasn't empty. The kitchen was to her right, complete with appliances, a full knife rack, and a mug waiting next to the sink. In front of her, a couple of comfortable-looking chairs faced a fireplace with built-in bookshelves on either side. A few nick-knacks and photos, more than you'd see in a magazine but not so much it was cluttered, lined the mantle and made an occasional appearance between the books on the shelves. Most of the books were hardbacks with embossed titles. An imperfectly folded newspaper lay on the small table between the chairs like someone had heard the doorbell ringing and had only meant to put it down for a few minutes. From the faint scent of aftershave and Aspercreme, but nothing feminine, she gathered the owner was an older male who had been gone for a few weeks or months but not years. The date on the paper confirmed it.

What had happened to him? Had he died? If the owner was dead, whoever had inherited the house could come by at any time. On the other hand, if he was ill and in the hospital or if he had moved to a senior-care facility, it might be awhile.

She only needed an hour, maybe. If she failed it wouldn't matter, not to her anyway. Maybe this wasn't a good idea. No one would want to come home to a dead body. Where else could she go though? Anyone, including wolves, could wander into an abandoned warehouse and for the same reason, caves were out of the question. Her friends would hide her but they might get caught in the curse too.

It was safer to do it here. She'd just have to pray she'd succeed and hope whoever owned the house would forgive her if she didn't.

After a quick inspection of her options, Honey chose the bedroom at the back of the house closest to the trees. If anyone came in any of the doors or drove into the empty garage, it would give her some time to get away or hide. Plus, it didn't feel right to sit in what was clearly the owner's bedroom.

She grabbed a couple of garbage bags to sit on, just in case things went really bad, then plopped down in the middle of the thin rug on the floor and pulled all fifty of the protection hair band charms she'd made onto her wrists and ankles. After a long talk with her parents and Jay and God, she made herself tug the box and the curse it held, out of the nether.

Either she was getting more sensitive or the curse was getting worse. She could sense it through the stone now. She put up the thickest magical shield she could muster and took off the lid.

Mr. No-Name's curse pulsed and writhed and banged around the inside of the box like a large knot of black snakes. Yuck. There would be no taming this spell with a simple pat to the head. How did someone tame a ball of snakes? A flute? A big net? Lot of sticks with hooks – none of which she had. All she had was magic blood.

Before she could poke herself, before she even transformed a single finger into a claw, the curse gave one last, big pulse, and blew up.

3

HONEY - NOVEMBER 18 - CURSE

Honey opened her eyes and checked her body. Despite the surge of power and air and things hitting her that she didn't want to think about, her body and her clothes were intact. The room, on the other hand, looked like it had been partially swallowed by a jungle. One corner and part of the roof had been completely replaced by trees. The opposite corner where the door had been was now a swampy lake complete with bugs. And, of course, snakes were everywhere. One of them sank its teeth into her ankle. For a brief moment, she thought she could feel them enter her skin, then she realized she was feeling the magic of her charm protecting her.

"Nope, not wasting that on you," she told the snake, then cut its head off with her claw. It vanished in a puff of smoke.

"It's all an illusion." She stabbed another snake that went for her arm. "I just have to find the veil and tear it down."

The problem was, everything looked real. If the snakes weren't so easy to dispatch, she'd think she truly had fallen asleep and ended up in some future time when nature was taking over. The trees were easy to dispatch too, as was the water, but they reappeared after a few minutes.

The natural light coming in through the window had faded to darkness by the time she thought to look outside.

17

The darkness was accompanied by growls and screeches from animals supposedly wandering in the night.

"Well, at least it's not a fire."

The moment she said it, a campfire popped up in front of her on the carpet/grass. It was a very nice little fire, perfect for a single camper with marshmallows and a hot dog.

She blinked at the food on the sticks now in her hands. "Okay, this is the strangest curse ever." Was it meant to lull her into a false sense of security or maybe the food would disappear as soon as she tried to eat it. She poked the hot dog with her claw. It disappeared into smoke just like the snakes. Was it poisoned? She tossed the sticks on the fire and looked around to see if the curse had cooked up anything else.

Several pairs of eyes, large eyes, blinked at her from behind the tree in the corner. Another set of eyes peered at her from the water.

More things to attack her. The curse was clearly meant to play on a person's fears, but the fears were easy to defeat. She killed all five of the creatures who attacked with one big swipe and two pokes. Was it meant to wear her out? She could see how witches who couldn't break spells would be at a disadvantage.

Another creature squeezed past the tree. This one had two legs, a smiling handsome face, and – a loincloth? Had they worn loincloths in England back in 1350 or whenever it was this curse was laid? The young man pointed to her fire, then himself, and smiled bigger. She waved her arm in a 'go ahead' gesture but didn't join him. She backed against the one untouched corner to think and watch. Before, she'd been able to rip the curse to shreds once she'd realized it was a curse. She knew this was a curse, but dragging her claws through the air did nothing because there was nothing to rip. Dragging them through the plaster on the wall did nothing either, except send dust into the air and allows thousands of spiders to pour into the room through the shallow grooves.

"Enough!" She waved her hand and pictured the spiders destroyed. Oddly, it worked.

"What is going on? Now I'm super-powerful?"

Loincloth guy looked up from whatever animal he'd started roasting over her fire and grinned. Even with the dirt smudged on his face and his shaggy, uncombed hair, he was cute.

She shook her head at him. "So weird."

He gestured at his food.

She shook her head again and slid towards the corner with the tree. Maybe outside would give her a clue.

It didn't. All she saw were the shapes of trees in the waning moon. Not knowing what else to do, she started walking. Monkeys welcomed her. Bears alternately attacked her or brought her honey. She finally tried a little, but it did nothing to ease her growing hunger. Night turned to day, then night again. She could feel herself weakening but she couldn't figure out what to do. The third night she found a cave and slept inside the dream. Nothing attacked her. She slept quite well, but when she woke she was so weak she didn't want to get up.

She stared up at the rough ceiling. "That's how it works. The curse weakens you until you give up, until you no longer want to wake up."

Wait a second, was she awake? She'd slept, but she was still in a cave that didn't exist. She pinched herself. She could feel pain and bleed, but she wasn't awake. Rainbow snakes didn't usually slither around and disappear when someone poked them.

It was a sleeping beauty curse, or something like it. She doubted anyone was supposed to kiss her awake. That meant she had to wake herself. How? Shouting at herself didn't work. Slapping her own face didn't either. All it did was make grinning loincloth boy appear again, except now it was more of a leer, like he was pleased about something that didn't bode well for her.

"You're Mr. No-Name," she realized. "Is that really how you picture yourself, like a boy in a loincloth?"

He looked down, appeared to realize for the first time what he was wearing, then looked up with a 'what are you going to do about it' look.

Why was he just now showing up again? What had she done? Was he here because she'd slapped herself? Was he supposed to distract her? If so, it meant she was right, she needed to wake up.

The boy started to untie his loincloth.

"Nope."

She froze him, then forced her weak body to stand and walk around him and leave the cave. He truly was frozen which meant her freezing power worked here. What if she froze the entire dream? If there was a noise or something in the real world, maybe it would stand out and she'd find a way to wake herself up.

Technically, freezing a dream should be impossible since there were no molecules, but since it was a weird curse-dream, she could apparently imagine all the molecules she wanted and how long they stayed still as evidenced by loin-cloth boy. She imagined a layer of ice over everything she could see and hear, including loin-cloth boy. From the mouth of the cave, which now looked out over a large plain, she watched the icy coating spread until everything was still. Even the birds soaring through the sky froze where they were. The world went silent with them. There was no more wind, no more odd roars, no more insects, just…wait. What was that roar – a car, a plane? It had to be. Nothing natural made that sound. What else? She sniffed the air. It smelled cold – no, go deeper – dust? That could be the cave. Herself? She sniffed her armpit. Yep. She sniffed it again, unfortunately, she was still in the mouth of the cave. She wasn't sure whether to be relieved or disappointed that her body odor wasn't strong enough to kick her awake. What about touch? She closed her eyes and reached out. Was she standing or sitting or laying down in real life? Was she still in the house? What if she was wandering down a road or lying in a creek? Stop it. Focus. Blank mind. No preconceived ideas. What did she feel? Cloth and … something smooth. It was big and … she opened her eyes and jerked her hands away. Loin-cloth guy had moved even though he was still frozen. Stupid curse.

Other senses. How about taste? She licked the back of her hand. Salty, but her mouth was so dry it felt like glue. Right, because she hadn't had a drink in three days dream time. She needed a drink, a real drink. She put out her hand and urged her magic to pull her backpack from the nether, her real backpack. She pulled the half-filled water bottle from her bag and chugged it down. It tasted like water. And…she was thirsty again like she hadn't drunk anything. Phooey. Something had to work.

Sight. She'd used her magical sight at first, but since

everything was a combination of the spell and her imagination, everything was wispy and molecule-free. Plus, it wasn't like she could look into her brain.

Wait a second. She *could* look into her brain. She could see her own molecules. How would she know they were real and not imaginary though? Shoot.

She was a curse-breaker. There had to be a way to break this curse. Her magic...right, her magic could do it. She was thinking too hard. She just had to want it.

"Come on. Get me out of here."

Nothing.

How did people normally wake up from dreams? She usually woke up because she was hungry (check) or thirsty (check) or needed to use the bathroom (check) or because she was about to die....

She looked around. Perfectly safe. Even when things were attacking her, she'd been safe because of her magic, but it wasn't really her magic because she was still in the dream. It was all an illusion.

Her head was starting to hurt.

"Okay dream, give me a deep, deep, like Grand Canyon deep, gorge right outside the cave. A beautiful gorge. I want to...paint it. A gorge with lots of colors."

She peered out of the cave. Everything looked the same.

"Tree climbing it is then."

Not too far away, a lone tree stood nearly twice as tall as everything else. In real life, she had no doubt a fall from the top would be deadly. She donned claws to start the climb up the limbless lower trunk and prayed the fall wouldn't be too painful in her dream.

The climb took hours, or at least it felt like it. Was the

spell trying to stop her or was she that weak? It had been so long since she'd eaten, her whole body was shaking by the time she made it to the top, especially her left foot.

This was it. She looked all around at the gorgeous landscape one last time, hoping for another answer, but nothing presented itself. She was either going to wake up, die, or somehow survive and still be in the dream. She looked down and her whole body clenched. There was no way she could survive this. She couldn't survive the dream much longer either though. Eyes wide open so she'd have the maximum scare, she jumped.

4

HONEY – NOVEMBER – SYDNEY

"It's about time. What the bloody hell are you doing in my house?"

Honey had to blink a couple of times before she could focus. A vine-free, tree-free ceiling was overhead. No snakes crawled on the bed to her right and no water feature blocked the door in the corner. The only thing odd was the glaring old man with an oxygen tube flowing to his nose whom she'd never seen before. He even smelled a little like an old man, but mostly of hospital.

This was real.

"Thank you, God," she said sincerely.

"Are you on drugs?" the man demanded.

"No. Sorry. I was stuck in that dream forever. Thank you for waking me up."

"What are you doing in my house?"

"I just needed a place to…a safe place to sleep for a little while," she said carefully. He was human. His house didn't have a hint of magic.

"So you chose my house?"

"It was empty and I didn't plan to stay long. What day is it?" It felt weird to be laying down with the old man looming over her. She pushed herself up and realized several things simultaneously. One, she really did need to use the bathroom, two, she was very sore from laying on the floor, and three, her stomach hurt, it was so empty.

"What did you take? Did you get into my medicine cabinet?"

"No! I didn't take anything. I really, really need to use the bathroom. May I use yours?"

"No!" he yelled. "I want you..."

A cough cut him off, and they kept coming. Her chest hurt listening to him. She rolled to her feet, forcing her stiff limbs to move, then put her arm around his shoulders to lead him to the bed. He resisted, but she pressed on.

"Sit down, so you don't knock into something. I'll get you some water."

He obeyed, slumping dejectedly on the edge of the bed. She rushed to where she remembered the kitchen was and filled up a glass from the tap.

His coughs had started to subside by the time she returned, but he didn't look good.

"You should rest."

He glared at her over the glass. "I would be resting if someone hadn't broken into my house."

"I'm sorry. I was desperate. I really didn't think anyone would be back. I figured whoever lived here had gone to an assisted living place."

"My daughter would like that," he huffed. "She acts like I'm ninety, not seventy."

"What happened?" She nodded toward the oxygen tank in the shoulder bag he was wearing.

"I caught a cold. My daughter insisted I go to the doctor. He insisted I check into the hospital where I caught pneumonia. What started as a three-day illness turned into nearly three weeks. Enough was enough. I checked myself out before I caught something else. Drove myself home. I'm never going to the hospital again."

The few times she'd stayed in the hospital weren't that bad. She'd liked Dr. Ziga and the nurses.

"Why? What was so bad about it?"

He snorted. "Someone was always popping into the room to check this or that, usually right after I'd finally got to sleep, unless I wanted something, then no one was around. The food was barely edible, the clothes were drafty, and there were too many people. I like my house and my neighborhood. They're quiet."

"I understand."

"Do you?"

She nodded. "Being around other people is hard sometimes. You have to watch what you say and do so they don't...get the wrong idea." Lame answer. She dropped her eyes to the ground so she didn't have to look into the man's piercing blue ones any more.

"What's in the box?" the man asked, nudging the stone with his foot.

She squatted down and peered inside. The gold brooch and the curse tablet were still there but the curse preventing her from destroying the tablet was gone.

What to tell him? She looked up at him so she could watch his face. "What do you know about curses?"

He raised an eyebrow. "Some people believe in them. I don't."

She pointed inside the box. "A long time ago, people used to write their curses on tablets, usually sheets of lead and bury them. That's what this is. When I opened the box, something inside went off. I fell asleep and got stuck in my dreams."

He frowned again. "Curse tablets were popular before Jesus, notably with the Greeks. Where did you find it?"

"Not here. Not in Australia, and this one is younger than that. There have always been some people who believe in magic."

He nudged the box again. "It looks old."

"I'm not sure when the box was made, but the tablet was made around 1350."

"How do you know?"

She glanced back down in the box. Was the silly thing safe to touch? It should be, but she was too weak to risk it right now. "I like to study history. I found mention of this tablet in a library and followed the clues to find it."

"It belongs in a museum."

"Maybe," she agreed noncommittally, "but there are more pieces. I need this one to find them." Very deliberately, she picked up the stone lid and placed it back on the box. "If I can't use your bathroom, I must go before something embarrassing happens. I didn't break anything when I came in, by the way, I picked the lock on your back door, and the only thing I touched was this floor."

"How old are you?" the man asked.

"I am a sophomore in college."

"That's not what I asked."

She shrugged but had to drop her eyes. He had the all-knowing teacher look down pat.

"You're all skin and bones. Are you a runaway?"

Not by choice, but he wouldn't understand.

"Do your parents know where you are?"

That she could answer.

"I assume so."

"You can't just assume. You have to call them occasionally and let them know you're okay," he scolded.

"Use my phone. Call them."

"I talk to them all the time." She pointed upward.

Understanding, then anger, or something akin to it appeared on his face.

"Can you cook?"

"Yes."

"Good. That bloody hospital wore me out. See what you can find in the kitchen. Use the bathroom at the end of the hall and take a shower. You reek. I'm going to take a nap."

"Thank you."

"Don't make me regret it."

5

HONEY - NOVEMBER 21? - SYDNEY

The moment the old man cleared the doorway, Honey sent the box to the nether, then headed for the bathroom. Behind the safety of the closed door, she pulled her backpack from the nether and immediately downed a bottle of water and a cliff bar, then retrieved her magic slates. The man had never told her what day it was, but maybe he didn't know either. Brayton's last frantic message was dated November 20, which meant today was at least the 21st. She erased his messages and added her own, hesitating over the 'Dear', but she'd kissed him and chosen him as her alpha, so ... still weird.

Dear BB, [17:40]
I'm okay. Got trapped in a spell but I'm awake now, I think. Not sure of the day. I'm in the home of an old man who just got back from the hospital. He asked me to cook for him. Since I broke into his house, it's the least I can do. - Wasp.

She grinned, thinking about Brayton's reaction to her breaking into a house, then caught sight of herself in the mirror. No wonder the man thought she was on drugs. Her eyes looked sunken and her cheeks and jawline had never been so prominent. She couldn't see her ribs through the loose T-shirt she was wearing, but she could feel them. No matter. A couple of gallons of water and a few good meals would fix her up.

Two hours later, she noticed the sun setting behind the trees from the kitchen window. Her watch was not wrong. It really was evening. That meant it was very, very early morning in Indiana. She turned off the stove and cracked the lid on the pot so her soup would cool faster. It had been months since she'd cooked a meal. She hoped it tasted as good as it smelled.

Should she wake the old man? Probably better to let him sleep since he had complained about people waking him.

There was too much soup for the old man to eat by himself even if he worked on it for a couple of days. She found a bowl in the cabinet and served herself. It tasted...good! A little salty, but there was only so much she could do with canned soup and vegetables. It didn't seem right to sit at the only spot with a place mat at the small two-person table. She made a second mat with a kitchen towel she found in the drawer and sat there.

She had just taken her third bite when someone banged – not knocked – banged on the front door. Should she answer it? Whoever it was had probably guessed someone was there since the kitchen light was on, and all that banging was going to wake the owner, if it hadn't already. What excuse could she give for her presence?

A dark shape leaned close to the wavy glass window by the side of the door like he or she was trying to peer in. Either they had a very strange hairdo, or they were wearing a cop hat. Someone, probably one of the neighbors, had called the cops. She could handle this.

With a blink, she pulled her blue contacts from the nether and donned the blond wig, hat, and hippie skirt.

Most people wouldn't wear a hat indoors, but she didn't have time to pull out her scarf and the cops would be able to tell she was wearing a wig if she didn't cover it with something.

She opened the door just as the angry woman cop was about to pound again.

"Yes?"

"Who are you?" the woman demanded.

"Lily," Honey answered automatically, doing her best to channel the now non-Scottish persona she'd created for the outfit.

"Where is my dad?"

The female cop had to be the sick man's daughter. She had the same grumpy look.

"Sleeping, or he was. You probably woke him, poor man."

"Poor man my ass," she said, storming past Honey. The aboriginal man with her, another cop, followed the woman inside. He paused and looked at Honey about the same time she realized he was a wolf. It might have been her imagination, but his eyes focused on her forehead under the hat instead of her face in that brief bit of time before he gave her a nod and moved past.

"What is that smell?" the woman demanded.

"Soup. You can have some if you're hungry. I made plenty."

The woman spun so that she was nearly nose-to-nose with Honey.

"Who. Are. You?"

"Lily."

"Why are you here?"

"Your dad asked me to cook for him."

31

"Bull's wool. My dad would never ask someone for help."

"Mikayla, leave my cook alone."

His daughter spun back around and jammed her hands on her ample hips. "Your cook? Since when do you have a cook?"

"Since I hired one." He sniffed the air. "Smell that? She did that with just what I had on hand. I had no idea anything in my pantry could smell that good."

"You can smell things now?"

"A little."

He still had the oxygen tube going to his nose. Honey wondered if he was lying for her sake, but she was too far away to smell if it was a lie.

"That's something at least. I can't believe you drove yourself home. You should have stayed another week."

"So I could catch something even worse and you could put me away and sell my house?"

"How many times do I have to tell you, I don't want your bloomin' house!"

"I know!"

His outburst instigated another coughing fit. Honey rushed into the kitchen and filled another cup with water, then stood silently by until he was able to take it.

He drank several sips then handed the glass back to her. "Thank you, Lily."

"You're welcome. Would you like to sit at the table or would you like me to make a tray for your room?"

"The table. Not too much. A cupful will be fine."

She rushed to do as instructed, being careful not to look directly at his daughter or her vengeful glare. She could feel both cops watching her as she put the man's soup on the table in front of him.

"I have some water heating too, if you'd like some tea. You have ginger and peppermint, which are both good for a cough, or I could make you some black tea with honey, which also helps."

"I'll take it black, no honey."

"Where did you find her?" Mikayla asked abruptly.

Her dad slowly slurped some broth from his spoon. "This is really good Lily. You should try some Mikayla. It reminds me of your mother's cooking."

"Answer the question Dad."

"She's a college student on a historical quest. She needs some financial help, so I thought I'd offer her a temporary job."

"Who introduced you?" she demanded.

"Mikayla, I'm a grown man. I was taking care of myself and avoiding thieves and crackpots long before you were born. Your input on my hiring choices is neither needed nor desired."

Mikayla squinted at him. "Dad, I'm a cop, I can tell when someone is hiding something. What are you not telling me?"

Her dad stuffed another bite of soup into his face. "Mmm good. So much better than that hospital crap."

Mikayla turned on Honey. "Show me your work visa."

"My work visa?"

"Since you aren't an Australian citizen, to legally work in Australia you need a work visa."

"How do you know I'm not a citizen?"

Mikayla folded her arms in front of her ample chest. "Prove it."

"Mikayla, leave her alone. She's only going to work

33

here a few days until I get better and I'm not paying her with money, I'm providing her with room and board," her dad said calmly.

Mikayla threw her hands up in the air. "I can't believe you! You never let me bring any friends over yet you invited a complete stranger to stay in your house with you?"

"She's a good cook."

Honey blinked back an unexpected tear. He was offering her a place to stay? That was remarkably sweet of him. What he needed though, was Mikayla off his case.

"If you want me to cook something other than soup, I'll need ingredients. Do you use a grocery delivery service or do you go to the store?"

"To the store. Dad's too cheap to use a service," Mikayla answered.

"I'll make a list then. Can you take me? I'm not used to your roads"

"In the police car?"

"I don't know what's legal here, but I do know your dad has a car, so maybe you could borrow it?"

"I'll take you," Mikayla's partner said.

"I asked her specifically to get her away from her dad," Honey told the partner. "The way she's going at him is wearing him out."

Predictably, her words didn't improve Mikayla's temper, but Honey hoped it was enough to get her to back off. Mikayla backed off right into Honey's face. "How dare you!"

"Mikayla," her dad snapped.

Honey raised her hand toward the man to show she had it handled. "It's okay, I understand. I'd be worried too if my dad was ill and he'd suddenly allowed some stranger to stay in his house and cook for him. Mikayla, I didn't ask him to hire me. I only cooked for him because I could tell he didn't feel well. I will leave if you wish, but at least let me shop for him. I had to throw out most of the things in the fridge."

"How did you meet?" she demanded.

"He, ah, woke me up. I fell asleep on his property."

"You were trespassing? You're a trespasser?" Her eyes bulged and her hand dropped to her belt.

"Don't you guys have wild camping here in Australia?" Honey asked as innocently as she could.

"No, and definitely not in people's yards!"

"Oh."

"Arrest her Cocogo."

"No," her dad said. "I don't want to press charges. I want her to cook for me and I want you off my property or I will call the coppers on *you*."

"Dad!"

"You don't want me here alone but when I find help you complain. You just want me out of my house."

Mikayla turned to crouch next to her father so that she was looking up at him and said in a softer voice, "No Dad. I want you to be safe. You should go back to the hospital where they can take care of you."

"There's nothing wrong with me that some rest and some good food won't fix. Lily will take care of me. Get back to work."

"Dad, this is ridiculous."

"Mikayla," her partner spoke up for the first time with an amazingly deep voice. "I know of Lily. She has a good heart. I'm sure she will do her best."

35

Honey focused in on Cocogo's face. He didn't look familiar at all. He caught her eye and tapped three fingers against his forehead. It was probably just her imagination, but her forehead tingled where Jay had kissed her. Cocogo was too wide to be the alpha with the stick, but maybe he was one of the other aboriginal wolves there the night of the full moon.

"You know her?" Mikayla punched Cocogo's arm. "Why didn't you say something sooner?"

Cocogo shifted his eyes to Mikayla and grinned. "It's fun to watch you going off like a frog in a sock."

"I am not...I can't believe you just said that. You're on reports the rest of the night."

"Sure pork chop," he emphasized the 'P' at the end of chop with a loud pop of his lips.

"I am not overreacting!"

"Lily," Cocogo said, focusing on Honey again. "Make your list. We'll pick up your supplies at the end of our shift."

"Thank you."

6

NOVEMBER 21 - NOVEMBER 22

Dear Wasp [Nov.21 5 am]

It's Thursday. You missed three check-ins. What spell? Are you safe? If I don't hear from you for 24-hours again, I'm coming out there.

Dear BB [Nov.21 22:00]

I'm safe. The man I told you about, I'll call him Al, has offered me free room and board if I cook and clean while he recovers from pneumonia. He's about 70 and his daughter is a cop. She doesn't like me, but I think her partner was there the other night and he spoke up for me. I made soup. Al seemed to like it.

Dear Wasp [Nov.21 6:29 am]

Do you think the wolves know what you are? What spell trapped you? Did you get the maps?

Dear BB [Nov. 22 8:30 am]

No to the maps, but I'm going to a library today that has them. The spell was what was protecting the artifact. It exploded and sucked me in. It's gone now. I made pancakes this morning. Al ate them, but he said they are called something else here and they're a little different. He very pointedly showed me his wife's cookbook. I put on a disguise when his daughter dropped by yesterday, but he hasn't asked about it. He thought I was doing drugs when he found me. I wonder what he thinks now.

Dear Wasp [Nov. 21, 11:35 pm]

Still weird to think it's already tomorrow afternoon where you are. Studying for a test. Wish you were here. You sure you're safe with Al? How did the library go?"

Dear BB [Nov. 22 22:12]

I found them! One is in Texas where we assumed, one is in South Africa, and one appears to be in the middle of the ocean. There are no islands in that region of the ocean. Either someone sank or they tossed their curse overboard. I don't know how we'll be able to reach the one in the water. There's probably a way though. I'll research it tomorrow. Al is okay. I made him a lunch before I left the house and made spaghetti with a salad for supper. I don't think he likes vegetables or salad. More for me.

Dear Wasp [Nov 22 9:55 am]

That's great news! I'm sure a certain girlfriend of yours will be glad to help with the travel arrangements. According to N, she visits a <u>lot</u>. Send me coordinates. About to take my test. WOLF was brutal this morning. I think I froze my claws off. Thanksgiving next week. Do you know how to cook a turkey?

7

BRAYTON – NOVEMBER 22 – INDIANA

"I thought you were staying this weekend," Rhys said as Brayton tossed his duffel back into the back of his SUV.

"I thought I was too, but Mom insisted she needed me at home," Brayton sighed, laying his backpack with his laptop down carefully beside his other bag.

"Those girls from the Little pack are going to be disappointed when you don't show up for country night tonight."

Brayton rolled his eyes. He hadn't mentioned his trip to see Honey to Rhys, but lately his stoic friend had found it strangely amusing to parade girls by and watch them fawn over him. Did he suspect something?

"I don't know why you want me to come. If I'm not there, they might notice you."

"Ouch. Fat-headed much?"

"I can't help if girls know a good thing when they see it."

Brayton slammed the door, missing whatever Rhys said in reply.

The sun disappeared behind the horizon just as Brayton rolled out of town. He turned up the radio and settled back into his seat for the drive. What was Honey doing right now? It was around 10 am in Australia, so perhaps she was in the library. How good could she cook?

Was Al regretting hiring her? Why had he hired her?

He knew she could take care of herself but being apart from her and pretending everything was normal, that he wasn't worrying about her nearly every minute of the day, was one of the hardest things he'd ever had to do. She was his Luna. He had every right to worry.

He noticed the flashing lights behind him right before he heard the siren. After double-checking the speedometer to make sure he hadn't zoned out and pressed the gas pedal too hard, he pulled to the side, fully expecting the cop to pass him. To his surprise, the cop pulled up behind him. Did he have a taillight out? He rolled down the window while simultaneously searching for his wallet.

"Brayton Mooney?"

He recognized the voice and was nearly certain it didn't belong to a cop.

"Damien?"

He looked right up into a powerful beam of light and smelled something odd. Where had all the dust come from? He blinked and the light vanished.

The next time he opened his eyes, a bright light was still blinding him, but it was bigger and brighter and there were two of them. He tried to lift his arms from where they were twisted uncomfortably behind him to shield his eyes, but he couldn't. He couldn't move his feet either. When he leaned to the side, he could just see metal bands around his ankles and the legs of the metal chair he was sitting on.

"Brayton Mooney."

The voice was feminine this time, and vaguely familiar. He ignored her and tried jerking his feet away from the chair again. The ties stayed whole and cut into his ankles through his jeans.

"Where is Honey Smith?"

He sniffed discretely. Magic, so a witch then. Something about her scent was irritatingly familiar. There was a wolf here too though – Damien, the traitor.

"Tell me where she is and I'll let you go."

She was telling the truth.

"Or don't and I'll use a spell to force the truth out of you. It's very painful or so I've heard, and some people aren't ever the same afterward, especially alphas."

Also the truth.

Was there any point in keeping quiet? Hell, yeah. No one was going to kidnap him and have it easy. How could he get out of this?

"Staying quiet will only bring you pain and possibly kill you," the witch said. "I don't want to kill you. I know your mother. She would be devastated, but that monster needs to be put down before something horrible happens."

A couple of months ago he would have told her that Honey wasn't a monster, but after telling and occasionally yelling it at his mother at least a hundred times, he knew the witch wouldn't listen. He closed his eyes against the bright lights and reviewed his options. It would be awkward, but he might be able to lean forward onto his toes enough to lift the back legs of the chair and spin around. If he could take out the witch, maybe he could talk some sense into Damien.

"You can't transform, if that's what you're thinking," the witch said. "I put a transformation inhibitor on you."

Only an inhibitor? That meant he could still use his alpha powers on Damien. Things were looking up.

"And don't think you can out-alpha me Brayton. I

have a protection charm," Damien said from the shadows.

Brayton kept his face and body as still as he could while wiggling his fingers behind his back to search the ties and the inhibitor bracelet around his wrist for weaknesses. They'd taken his ring. Darn.

"The girl is only one person Brayton, one person. There are hundreds of thousands of wolves and witches whose lives are going to be ruined because of her," the witch tried.

He couldn't take the stupidity. He lifted his head to stare at the origin of the voice. "Name one."

"Well, you."

"Do I look ruined?"

"The girl's parents."

"They lived just fine for fourteen years. If Honey was cursed they would have died much earlier."

"Gaian Graves."

"What?" He hoped she could see how stupid that was from the look on his face. "In what way?"

"He went crazy. He wouldn't have attacked you otherwise. The curse made him go crazy once he knew what she was."

It was understandable she didn't know the whole story. Gaian hadn't been tried for the murders, yet.

"He's the one who killed her parents before he even knew she existed. The curse wouldn't have been active on him then."

"You're wrong."

Typical.

"Oh, I'm sorry, did you also almost get your face burned off by a man with a vendetta against a girl simply because her mom chose another man over him? My bad."

"You don't know what you're talking about."

"Clearly, because I have never talked to the girl, or lived in the same house with her, or gone to school with her. She saw them burn you know."

"There. See. Proof. That was the curse working."

The witch was just like Mom. Impossible.

"Go ahead and use your spell on me. I'm not going to tell you a thing either way because I don't know the answer and when they discover you've used magic on me, you'll be imprisoned just like Gaian."

"Liar. I know you're in contact with her," the witch said triumphantly. Something flickered through the light and landed in his lap. The magic slate, he realized with a sinking heart. They'd found it. Now he'd have no way to communicate with Honey at all. She'd written to him again. He had to twist his head to read the upside-down words.

Dear BB [Nov 23, 21:01]

They don't have Thanksgiving here silly. These are in code. I'll tell you how to convert them in my next message: 79.~~4458682274--4(SA), 69.151941, R73.645924(AO), we know the other. You should write them in code in case they're stolen. Al's daughter followed me to the library today. I ditched her after I was done and went on a run. She was hacked when she showed up at dinner time and I was serving her dad meatloaf (he requested it). He said it was perfect, but I think he was egging his daughter on. How was your test?

"Why does she call you BB?" Damien asked.

"Where did you find this?" Brayton countered.

"In your backpack," Damien said.

"Huh."

"Stop. I know that's from her to you. I've seen you with her. You're tail-over-snout for her, plus that's what she called you on her phone too," Damien said.

"You saw what was on Honey's phone?"

"Your mom turned it in a long time ago," the witch said. "What are those numbers for?"

"What do you think they're for?"

The witch darted forward and slapped him. It felt like a five-year-old had tapped his cheek compared to the punches he took sometimes. He smirked at the witch where she'd sank back into the shadows shaking her hand.

"Who's Al?" Damien asked.

Brayton shrugged.

"This is getting us nowhere. We need to use the spell," the witch said.

"No," Damien said. "Let me talk to him. He just needs some convincing."

"Fine, you have half-an-hour," the witch said too readily.

They'd planned this.

Brayton heard footsteps going up and then the click of a door shutting. It was only then that Damien started to speak. Brayton cut him off.

"Do you mind turning off the lights? I know who you are. And if you're planning on beating the answers out of me, you'll want them off. They give off a lot of heat."

"Better I beat you than what she's got planned for you," Damien said even while he switched off the lights. "I don't want to hurt you though. I consider you a friend. Just tell me where Honey is and I'll get you out of here."

It took several long moments for Brayton's eyes to

44

adjust, especially his new eye. As he'd suspected from the smell and the chill, they were in a room with cement walls, probably a basement. The only light came from the top of a stair-well behind Damien. Brayton blinked twice to survey his surroundings for spy-spells. He was used to seeing them, but the big, wolf-sized one with spy-dish ears and kangaroo feet next to Damien was startling. That's why the smell of the witch irritated him. She was the source of the spy spells.

"What?" Damien said, looking to where Brayton was looking.

Brayton tore his eyes away from the strange creature. "Thought I saw something moving. Probably a rat." Damien didn't know about his eye's magical abilities and he was never finding out now. "You realize the witch will have a way to spy on us, right? If you were thinking of double-crossing her, she'll hear whatever you hear."

"I have no reason to do that. She's promised me they'll get Honey to break the spell on me."

"And how are they going to do that? Honey doesn't do anything she doesn't want to."

"A curse-breaker doesn't have to be alive to break curses."

He'd known Damien wasn't the greatest guy, but that was a whole different level of low. Anger stronger than anything Brayton could remember feeling flooded him. If Damien wasn't wearing a protective charm, he'd be on the ground bowing, with his forehead on the floor from the alpha power Brayton could feel pouring from him.

"You would use the blood from her dead body?" His voice came out low and dangerous, nothing like his normal one. If he hadn't been so mad, he would have scared himself.

Damien took a step back. "I wouldn't be the one to kill her."

Brayton had never wished so hard in his life that his eyes could shoot lasers, real ones. Unfortunately, he hadn't even managed to shoot magic ones with the magical eye yet.

"Beyond how wrong that is in principle, the witches are wrong in general. I saw Honey after she broke a curse. She passed out and slept for over a day. It takes a lot of power and effort. If you let them kill her, you'll never get that spell broken."

"Please Brayton, tell me where she is. I just want her to remove the spell."

"Damien, you're a fool. She's running for her life. You can't just go visit her. The witches are following all of us. You would lead them right to her."

"She could just portal away again. It would only take a moment for her to break the spell."

Brayton wanted to shake Damien until his selfish head popped off its neck and rolled across the floor, preferably into the large spider web in the corner. "Portals cost $1000 and the witches aren't allowing wolves to buy them anymore. Why should she use one on you?"

"My dad is sick. I'm pretty sure my brother is taking his power too. If my dad loses his power, he'll have no choice but to declare Deacon alpha."

After what Alpha Meyer did to Zavier and after siccing his twin sons on Honey, Brayton didn't feel sorry for Damien's dad in the least. "Even if Honey broke the spell, you wouldn't have enough power to beat Deacon," he pointed out.

"But I would have some. Enough to be beta."

"Is that my ring?" Brayton asked, noticing the familiar object on Damien's finger.

Damien shrugged. "Finders' keepers."

Jerk. As soon as he figured out how to get loose... wait, maybe he could trick Damien into disabling his protection charm.

"Um, you've got something crawling up the front of your shirt."

Damien looked down instead of swiping, but he could work with that.

"I don't see anything."

"It jumped up to your neck. Can't you feel it crawling on your skin?"

Damien looked up and shook his head. "I can smell you're lying."

Brayton kept his eyes on the imaginary bug and shrugged. "Um, okay." He shifted his eyes downward like he was watching the bug walk to Damien's collar, then looked up after he imagined it walking under his collar.

Damien ignored him. "How often does she write to you?"

"There really is something under your shirt." A charm, for instance, assuming Damien was wearing it on that chain around his neck. If he could just convince him to tap it with the ring...

"Stop playing games and answer the question."

"Are you more susceptible to spider bites since you lost your alpha powers?"

Damien glared at him.

Brayton moved his eyes back to Damien's collar. "Because if not, maybe you're not more susceptible to anything else either."

"Where is Honey?" Damien half-yelled.

Damien's arm twitched like he wanted to do something with it. Brayton pretended he didn't notice and continued watching his imaginary bug.

"Any luck," the witch asked from half-way up the stairs as if she didn't have a big spy-spell watching and listening to everything.

"Not yet."

"He's not going to talk to you," the witch said, jogging down the wooden stairs to stop by Damien's side. "His mom has been working on him for months." She lifted up the object she held in her hand for Brayton to see. It looked like a cross between a crown and a tiara that had been roasted black in a fire and slightly melted. The magic around it made it look like it was still burning. "Last chance Brayton. This crown has made grown men cry and beg. The more you refuse to answer, the more pain it causes."

He really, really wished he had practiced more with the eye laser. All he had to do was let himself have it. Come on, nice strong laser to obliterate the spell.

"What are you doing Brayton?" Damien said, "You look constipated."

"I don't suppose you'll let me go to the bathroom before we get started?"

"No," the witch said. "There's a drain in the floor. It will be easy enough to clean up whatever leaks after we're done."

That didn't sound promising.

8

BRAYTON – NOVEMBER 22 – INDIANA

The witch pressed the rough, uneven edge of the black crown thing firmly onto Brayton's head, then stepped back looking pleased. "Finally, we'll get some answers. Where is Honey?"

"Honey who?"

A fierce pain that reminding him strongly of the headache he'd had for weeks after drinking the spelled beer last year stabbed into his brain. For a moment he thought he might throw up, then the pain was gone. That wasn't so bad.

The witch nodded, clearly pleased. He must have made a face. He wouldn't give her the satisfaction a second time.

"Hurts, doesn't it? Let's try that again. Where is Honey?"

He chose not to answer. Might as well test the spell out. The pain started slowly, as if the crown was reminding him to answer. The longer he waited, the more the pain grew. He wasn't sure how fast it escalated, but it seemed to take at least a minute to go from mild headache to railroad nail through the temple. By then he couldn't answer since opening his mouth would no doubt mean emptying his stomach. This was worse than the beer, but not worse than getting his skin burned off. How bad would it get before he passed out or would the spell keep him awake? There was no way anyone could survive this pain if it was real. Maybe this was an illusion spell. Yep, all an illusion. His brain was not frying, not frying, not frying.

"Hey, Brayton, you still in there?"

Was the worry in Damien's voice because he was concerned for him or because he didn't want to get in trouble? The force with which he was slapping Brayton's cheeks suggested the latter. Brayton rolled his head back partially to make him stop and partially to relieve the kink. How long had he been out?

"Brayton, that was painful to watch. Just tell the witch what she wants to know and I'll take you home myself."

Damien's voice was lower than it should be for his height. Brayton cracked an eye open. He was still in the basement and still in the chair, but if he moved fast, he might be able to ram Damien in the face, which was just below his level, or maybe do the spin he'd thought of earlier. Lunging was easier. Unfortunately, Damien sensed his plan, because he sprang out of the way, leaving Brayton to land nearly face-first on the cement. He did manage to turn slightly so his shoulder got the worst of it. At least he was laying down now.

Damien hauled him back upright. "That was stupid. Now she'll know you can handle another go."

The second time around with the crown was worse. It must have been testing him the first time, because the bad pain started earlier and lasted longer when he refused to talk. By the third time around he wasn't sure he *could* talk anymore. Did it make sense to stay silent, he asked himself when the witch lowered the crown on him the fourth time.

Honey would escape, she was amazingly adept at slipping away. It wasn't like he could tell them exactly where she was. A picture of a dart floated through his jumbled brain. He'd caught her once. If the people after her shot and drugged her, she'd be at their mercy. He couldn't let that happen, not to his Honey. If he died though, the witch would probably go after her friends next. They knew as much as he did and they had the other slate. She'd truly be all alone with no one to communicate with. He had to warn her. He knew it was too far, but they had a connection. He'd felt it form when she'd chosen him as her alpha. He had to get a message to her even if he died trying.

9

HONEY – NOVEMBER 24 – SYDNEY

Honey took a shower, then checked the magic slate one more time. Why hadn't Brayton written? His last message had been on Friday morning. It was now, she did the calculation in her head, Sunday morning his time. He'd never missed writing to her before. Something was wrong.

The boys' slate was still blank. Did that mean they were in trouble too, or did they not realize Brayton was?

Still in her towel, she pushed the dresser by the door over a couple of inches to prevent the door from opening without warning. Mr. Helman had never walked in on her, but she didn't trust Mikayla not to try it one day.

Where could Brayton be? Should she pop directly to him or to one of her friends? Was there any point in disguising herself? She pulled her options out of the nether. If he was in trouble, or even stuck at home, a disguise might make someone hesitate to attack. She pulled on black sweats, a dark gray, oversized hoodie, and her balaclava, but didn't pull the bottom part all the way up. She had to leave her lips free because…, her stomach tingled.

"Stop that," she whispered at it firmly.

Forming a lip-to-lip tether hadn't been one of her better ideas. Speaking of tethers, she put the back of her bare hand against the wall in her room. It would be really stupid not to have a way back.

She made sure all her other belongings were tucked safely in the nether, her shield bands were on her wrists, her I'm-a-witch charm was pinned to her bra, and her air shield was in place, then hesitated. What if he was in bed, or worse, the shower or the bathroom? He was probably fine. She was being paranoid.

"Honey, you must go."

Was she imagining things now too? That sounded just like Brayton – a Brayton in pain.

"They're going to torture your friends to find you."

That *was* Brayton.

"I didn't talk. I love you."

Didn't. That was past tense. No. She wasn't going to lose Brayton too. She took a deep breath and dived into the nether.

10

DAMIEN – NOVEMBER 24 – WITCH'S HOUSE

Brayton's head rolled forward and dropped to his chest again, he was still awake though. His moans and the reek of his anguish along with his urine were still perfuming the air. The scent made Damien simultaneously want to rip Brayton free and help him or get himself far, far away. Hilda the witch, on the other hand, didn't appear affected at all. He should have never agreed to act as her lie detector. Why was Brayton so stubborn? All he had to do was name a place and they could all go about their business.

"Maybe there's something wrong with the spell," Hilda muttered for at least the tenth time.

"There's nothing wrong with the spell, you just underestimated how stubborn Brayton can be."

"There are other things we can try. I won't be able to access them until tomorrow morning though. What time can you get here?"

"Not until evening. I have to work."

"That's fine. It will give me time to prepare."

"Prepare for what?"

"The blood."

Damien glanced at her to see if she was kidding. It didn't look like it. "Don't you have a spell that will just force him to talk instead of torturing it out of him?"

She shrugged. "They exist, but I don't have one. Besides, this way he learns a lesson too. He is not all that, as you younger people say."

"I have never used that phrase, nor have I heard anyone else use it."

Movement had him turning back towards Brayton. A person all in black crouched beside him. Where had they come from? The only way in or out was the stairs. Whoever it was had already removed the ugly black crown from Brayton's head.

"Stop!" Hilda yelled.

The person tilted his or her head up just long enough for Damien to see black where the cheek should be before the crown was flying toward him like an evil Frisbee. He dove to the side. When he looked back up, Brayton and the person in black were gone.

"Who was that?" Hilda demanded.

"I don't know."

"Male, female?"

"I couldn't tell."

Hilda looked at him doubtfully. "With your nose, you couldn't tell?"

"Brayton's stench pretty much overwhelms everything."

"True," she agreed.

He really didn't like that woman.

"What now?

"Now we wait and see what turns up. I stuck a tracking spell on Brayton just in case he escaped."

He had to give credit where it was due. "Smart."

"Indeed. If that was Honey, he's just led us right to her."

11

HONEY – NOVEMBER 24 – SYDNEY

"Brayton, Brayton, talk to me," Honey whispered, lifting his head from where it sagged forward on his chest. His skin was pale and thin like he'd been ill for a long time and his body reeked of urine and sweat, but not the good kind of sweat that came from exercise.

He moaned. Usually moaning wasn't a good sign, but she'd take it since it meant he wasn't dead.

"I'll get you out of this."

She touched the metal bands around his ankles and wrists, sending them to the nether. Red, oozing stripes where the sharp metal had cut into his skin remained. "Oh, Brayton."

Without his arms strapped around the back of the seat, he slumped forward and would have fallen if she hadn't zipped around the chair to catch him.

"Brayton. I'm sorry. I'm sorry you had to suffer because of me."

He sighed on her shoulder.

"Can you walk?"

His body sagged closer to the floor.

"No matter. Here. You can lay right here." She lowered him gently onto the thin carpet. "I'll get you cleaned up, then I'll make you a nice, soft bed with my sleeping bags."

She carefully pushed the dresser back into place and

stuck her head out in the hallway. Everything looked just like it had a few minutes ago and Mr. Helman was already snoring. Good.

"I'll be right back," she whispered toward Brayton, then slipped into the hall.

She knew the basics of how to give a person a sponge bath thanks to one of the nurses who had cared for Zavier, and with her magic he was easy to undress. She didn't give him a full sponge bath, just enough of one that he'd feel more comfortable and wouldn't make her sleeping bags stink.

"There," she said, surveying his towel-covered form. "Feel better?"

He shivered.

"Yeah, you're right. You should get the bed." She eyed the distance between him and his destination. "Think you can help me?"

He didn't even moan. What had they done to him? The brief sniff she'd taken of the spell on his head before she'd broken it had made her think of every torture device she'd ever heard of. The molecules in his head looked like they were going the right way but they were…agitated, no that wasn't quite right…angry, no…over-stimulated, maybe. She moved the bowl of water to the side, turned down the sheets, then pulled Brayton over her shoulder in a fireman's carry. He was a lot heavier than Rosemary, her friend at the Canadian climbing center with whom she'd practiced once on a whim.

"Better?" she asked a few minutes later after the towel was back around his waist and he was all tucked in.

He buried his nose in her pillow. "Honey."

"I'm here."

"Talk I didn't. I talk can't. They find would you."

"I'm here. They didn't find me. You did good."

He pulled her pillow into a hug. "Hurt. Over and over. Wouldn't stop they. Have I them couldn't let you. My Luna you're."

"No, no, Brayton don't cry. I'm here. I'm here. I won't let them hurt you again," she rubbed his shoulders through the blanket. They'd made Brayton cry – big, strong bully Brayton, a future alpha, no, an alpha already, her alpha. And his tears were making her cry. What had they done to him?

"Hold on. I'll be right back."

She scooted the dresser back in front of the door, then lay down on the covers beside him and curled around his back. She hadn't managed to get his clothes into the washer. They'd just have to wait.

12

HONEY – NOVEMBER 25 – SYDNEY

"Lily, are you in there?"

Honey startled awake with the smell of Brayton in her nose and a warm lump under the covers next to her. Shoot, she must have fallen asleep. She rolled off the top of the covers and padded over to the door.

"Yes. Sorry, Mr. Helman. I overslept. I'll get started on breakfast right away. Just give me a few minutes."

"That's all right. I'm up early. My daughter just called me. She won't be able to drive me to my appointment and she suggested you do it."

"Why me? I've never driven in Australia. Wouldn't it be safer to drive yourself?"

"They say you're not supposed to drive after they dilate your eyes."

"That's nice she trusts me but…it's a trick," Honey realized.

"What?"

"She's planning on pulling me over so I'll have to show her some ID."

"You're probably right," Mr. Helman said after a short pause. "Do you have an ID?"

Honey pushed the dresser to the side and opened the door so she could see his face. "Not with my current name and blond hair."

"Hmm." He wrinkled his nose. "What is that smell."

She'd gotten used to the stench of Brayton's laundry overnight. It must be really bad if Mr. Helman could smell it. She momentarily tried to think of a way to hide Brayton then discarded the idea. She couldn't keep Brayton from Mr. Helman, not when he'd been so kind to her and it was his house.

"Last night, I rescued a friend. He was being tortured. I brought him here because I knew it was safe." She stepped aside and gestured at the bed.

"Tortured? Who was torturing him?" Mr. Helman walked in and looked down at the back of Brayton's head, then around the room at the bowls of water still on the edge of the carpet and the pile of clothes on the hardwood.

"The people looking for me. They were trying to get him to say where I was. Don't worry, he didn't say. He couldn't since he didn't know."

"Why are people looking for you? Are you involved in something illegal?"

"No! Nothing like that."

How to put it so he would understand without revealing anything? "You know how some pale people don't like people with dark skin?"

"You mean whites and blacks?"

"Yes, and say, Nazis and Jews?"

"Yes."

"It's like that."

He blinked at her very deliberately. "You have neither dark skin nor are you Jewish, are you?"

"No. Those were examples."

"Who's chasing you and why?"

She shook her head. "I can't tell you. Let's just say my

parents were from two different secret societies and the fact that they got together and had me made both sides mad."

"Sounds like a movie I watched once."

"How did it end?"

He started coughing before he could answer. Honey retrieved the still unused cup of water from the little table by the bed and offered it to him.

After a few sips he said, "I don't remember. What are you going to do with him?"

"I'd like to get him back to his parents but it might take me a few days to arrange things. Can he stay here?"

"What will you do if I say no?"

"We will leave."

"You drive a hard bargain. I suppose I should ask before I agree, what will they do to me if they find you?"

"Nothing. You're an outsider, an innocent, someone I used. They might ask you questions, but just tell them the truth. There's nothing about me that you have to hide except my current location, which, if they are questioning you, won't be here."

"Mm." He handed the water back to her. "I don't think the eye doctor will appreciate me coughing in his office. I'll cancel. Why don't you make some breakfast and throw your friend's clothes in the wash. Does he have anything else to wear?"

"I'll find him something if he wakes up."

"Does he need a doctor?"

She looked back over at Brayton. The way he was still curled around the pillow didn't seem like Brayton at all. "Maybe, but not for anything physical."

"Ah. Well, I'll see you in the kitchen."

13

BRAYTON – NOVEMBER 25 – WITH HONEY

Bacon. He sniffed the air again. That was bacon. Where was Honey? Had he dreamed her? No. The pillow in his arms smelled of her. Where was she? He had to make sure she was safe. A girl's voice – Honey's, and a man's voice. Was she in danger? He followed her smell and the smell of bacon down a short, dark hallway. There, at the stove. She looked fine. The old man was sitting and too far away to harm her. She was cooking. His Honey could cook.

His stomach cramped. When was the last time he'd eaten? Not since, it was hard to remember. Something about a car and flashing lights.

"Brayton? Ack! Why are you naked? I left you some clothes."

She wouldn't look at him. Funny Honey, always so squeamish about being naked in front of other people. Something like a laugh escaped him right before he swiped a piece of bacon off the plate next to the stove. She really could cook.

"Brayton stop eating all the bacon. That's for Al."

"Cook good."

"Go put the clothes on and I'll make you a plate."

"Here you'll be?"

She nodded, with her eyes firmly on the pan. Funny Honey.

"He's not moving," a man's voice said.

A warm hand touched his arm, sending shivers down his back. "Brayton, what's wrong."

"I you leave can't. Hurt they you."

"They aren't here. Now we are having breakfast and you have to put clothes on to eat."

"Leave can't."

"Okay, you stand there and let me serve Al, then I'll go with you to get the clothes."

"Why are you calling me Al," the man asked.

"Because if he doesn't know your real name he can't tell anyone."

Logical Honey.

"Why is he talking like Yoda?"

"I don't know. I think whatever they did to him scrambled his brain a little."

Smart Honey.

"He's well-endowed."

"Stop please."

"Very fit."

"Stop looking at him."

"Reminds me of me when I was young."

"I did not need to know that."

Innocent Honey.

"Here you go. Your coffee should be ready shortly."

"Thank you, Lily."

"Honey," Brayton corrected him.

"Honey does not taste good in coffee," his helpful Honey said, grabbing his elbow. "Let's get you dressed.

63

Actually, you should take a shower first. I'll show you where it is."

"Me with stay?" he pleaded when she released his elbow in front of a door.

"I'm not taking a shower with you. I'll wait right here though after I get the clothes."

He leaned over and kissed one of the three dots he could see shimmering on her forehead. "Love I you."

"Go."

He couldn't see or smell Honey in the shower. He rubbed soap all over himself, spun around under the water, and was done.

To his relief, Honey was where she said she'd be.

"Brayton, you have to wash the soap off. Close your eyes, the soap is about to run into them. Come on, I'll stay with you."

She wiped his face then started the water again. He wanted her in the shower with him, where he could keep an eye on her. She shut the shower curtain. He immediately opened again.

"Shut the curtain Brayton. I'm not going anywhere. We can talk. Tell me what happened."

He opened his mouth and thought for a long time, but the only word he could pull up was, "Pain."

"I'm sorry Brayton. Let's try this. You sit down and I'll finish washing your hair for you, then you can rinse, okay."

Honey was going to touch his head? "Okay!"

She laughed. He'd made his sad Luna laugh!

"You're like...what am I going to do with you?"

He grinned at her from where he now sat in the tub, hoping, hoping, yes! Her lips landed softly on his. He was careful not to push back, to let her have control. He didn't want to scare her.

Her lips left his too soon, but her forehead still leaned against his. As long as she was close it was enough.

"I missed you."

That definitely needed another kiss. His turn.

"You are very good at that," she breathed softly when he finally ended it.

Not trusting himself to say anything sensible, he grinned.

"Okay, let's get you clean."

14

HONEY – NOVEMBER 25 – SYDNEY

She shouldn't be kissing him, not when he wasn't himself, but every time he gave her that look, both yearning and teasing, she couldn't help herself. She pulled Jay's shirt over Brayton's head and kissed him again. His arms shot through the sleeves and she was wrapped in his damp, finally clothed warmth.

Brayton's hugs weren't like the guys' hugs. His were more…electric.

"Okay, enough," she pushed away. "You need food. Your stomach has been talking almost non-stop since you woke."

He nodded and indicated she should depart the small bathroom first.

Mr. Helman was still at the table, although his plate was clean and his coffee cup empty. "I was beginning to wonder if you'd drowned in there."

Considering how wet her front now was, it wasn't a poor assumption. "No. He needed assistance. Do you want more coffee?"

He held his cup up to her. "Please."

"Brayton, sit. I'll make you something."

"Bacon."

"Yes, bacon."

"Where did you find clothes that could fit him?" Mr. Helman asked.

"Oh, I had them. They belonged to a friend of mine."

She glanced at Brayton to see his reaction, but couldn't tell what he was thinking with his eyes closed as they were.

"Brayton, are you okay?"

He nodded.

He looked okay. Not knowing what else to do she turned back to the counter. "We need more eggs. This is the last of them."

"I can drive you," Mr. Helman said.

"You sure? I don't mind walking."

"That's a long walk."

She nodded. She didn't have time to walk. She needed to take Brayton home or at least tell his dad what had happened and that he was okay and warn her friends they might be tortured and then find a new country to stay in. So much to do. What she really needed to focus on was finding the other three curses. Maybe she could go to South Africa next. She had one portal left. If she went home through the nether and warned the boys, she could use the portal to get to South Africa, then nether back to the US. She'd need to go to the library first though and do some research so she knew what to focus on when she portalled to South Africa.

It was Sunday evening in Indiana. If she waited a few hours, it should be safe to visit Walter since he would be in bed.

She turned on the burner under the bacon pan and started cracking the eggs into a bowl. "I have to go, Mr. Helman. Will you be okay?"

"I'll be fine. I feel much better. You took good care of me. Where are you going to go?"

"You know I can't say. I'll clean up before I go."

67

"Go I you with," Brayton declared.

"Yes," she agreed.

"Will you come back?" Mr. Helman asked.

"Unlikely."

Mr. Helman's cell phone rang from his shirt pocket. Honey tried not to listen, but his daughter was anything but quiet even when she was trying to talk softly.

"Dad, is that woman still there?"

"Yes. We're eating breakfast."

"Send her out of the house."

"Why?"

"She's a murderer Dad."

Honey could feel Mr. Helman's eyes boring into the back of her head while she turned the bacon.

"Who?"

"At least ten people. Old people, like you."

"How do you know it's her?"

"They have her name and your address."

That was impossible, unless...Honey looked back at Brayton who was frowning at Mr. Helman. Brayton wouldn't have said anything. He hadn't had the time or opportunity. Spy spells, she realized when she switched to her molecular sight. How had she not smelled them? With a surge of molecules, she destroyed the little long-necked monster standing by Mr. Helman's side and the other three smaller spells she detected in the room, then turned back to the stove.

The food was basically done. She turned off the burners and scooped the food onto the waiting plates.

"Here Brayton," she sat his plate in front of him. "Eat fast. I want to visit the library before we leave."

He tapped his magic eye. She nodded.

"Okay. It might be a few minutes," Mr. Helman said.

"Just send her out."

"Patience, Mikayla." He fiddled with the phone a few moments, then set it face down on the table. "That was my daughter," he said with a sigh.

"I gathered."

"Have you ever," he shook his head and looked down into his cup. "She bought some groceries but she doesn't want to come in. Can you get them?"

"Sure." She sent her shoes, which were out of his sight under the table, to the nether. "Just let me get my shoes. Come on Brayton, let's get your shoes too. You can help me carry in groceries."

Brayton shoved the last of his eggs into his mouth, then grabbed his toast. She handed him hers, then put their plates on the counter. Did Mr. Helman really believe she'd killed people? She'd thought he'd trusted her at least a little. Why were people so eager to believe lies?

"Mr. Helman, thank you for your hospitality. Just so you know, the only crime I've ever committed is breaking into your home, well that and a library, but that was just to look something up. The people after me know that, but they don't care."

He looked up from his coffee cup, older than she'd ever seen him. "They're..."

She cut him off. "It's okay. I've got this. You get better, okay?"

She vanquished another two spy spells in the hallway and another in the bedroom. Had they seen her and Brayton kissing? Probably. Well, their relationship wasn't that big of a reveal since Brayton had spoke on her behalf from the beginning. She popped into her Lily costume while Brayton put on his shoes. She needed a new disguise.

The room still smelled faintly of Brayton's clothes, but more telling was the smell of metal which she was certain was meant to block her from using a portal. Weren't they going to be surprised.

"Ready?"

He walked into her open arms and nodded.

"Hold your breath."

15

BRAYTON – NOVEMBER 25 – CAVE

He wasn't sure what he expected, but it wasn't this. It looked like…a cave? Honey sighed and let go of him then walked toward what the light suggested was the entrance.

"Are where we?"

Darn it. Why wouldn't his words come out right? They sounded fine in his head.

She held up her hand with the sign he'd taught her for silence and peered around a stone corner toward the source of the light, then slipped past it. He was about to follow her when she stepped back inside.

"Looks clear."

"Did where go we?"

"You mean where did we zip to before here?"

He nodded.

"That was the nether. Don't ever send yourself there. You have to be tethered to something here on Earth to get back and I don't think you can breathe there."

He touched his lips and pointed to hers.

"Yes, exactly. I also put an anchor here one day in case I needed a quick getaway. I made a mistake. I should have thought to check for bugs on you."

"Spell spies?"

"Yes. I saw several in the kitchen when I looked for them. That's how they knew where we were."

Brayton blinked twice and checked the cave himself,

then saw her. She was lit up with a white glow, just like the moon.

"Why are you staring at me?" she asked him.

"Glow you."

"Don't other witches and wolves glow?"

He shook his head.

"I bet it's my protection spells." Her eyes went wide and she ran to his side and grabbed his wrist. "They could be scrying you right now. You'll have to stay close to me until I can get you to…," she looked around, "let's keep moving, just in case."

"Where?" he asked once they were on the faint trail near the cave.

"Walter," she whispered. "He can take you to your dad so you can get someone to help you and I can tell him where the other curses are."

"No. Everywhere spies."

"I can destroy them."

"No talk time to. You catch."

Ugh, that made no sense at all.

"You mean they'll catch me? I'll bring Walter here," she continued after he nodded.

"Waiting go you back when." No sense. He growled at himself.

Honey, contrary thing that she was, grinned at him. "You do sound like Yoda."

"Funny not," he huffed.

She patted his shoulder and sighed, making him feel bad. He should have let her tease him.

"I know," she said. "Your brain looks fine, just irritated. I think it will get better. If not, my grandmother should be able to help."

He lifted the hand he was holding and kissed the back of it. "No back go. You, me," he squeezed her hand.

Brayton, you can't stay with me. You have to finish out the semester."

He pointed at his mouth. "This like?"

"I'm sure you'll be fine in a few days."

"Torture what if again me?"

"You'll know to be careful now."

Her words lacked conviction. She was weakening.

"Thanksgiving. Stay I."

"Your mom will be worried sick."

"Mom worry can," he grumbled.

"You don't mean that. Your mom loves you. Besides, I'm sure your dad will worry too."

"Idea," he blurted.

"What?" Honey asked as if blurting out that you had an idea was totally normal.

"Write. Dad. Note."

"That was better," she nodded encouragingly.

"Deliver you. Fast."

"To Walter?"

He nodded. "Fast. Pop, pop. Quiet. Leave note just."

"Okay."

"Dad. Office. Protected."

"Right. You told me that. If we address the letter to your dad and specify his office, maybe say it can only be read there, Walter will deliver it and they can read it together."

"Yes!"

She grinned. "Just think how much more challenging this would be if you couldn't talk at all."

He growled at her, and she immediately sobered and

73

looked away. "Sorry. I...that came out wrong. I was trying to be encouraging."

He could literally feel her pulling into herself. He elbowed her and flashed her a toothy grin. "Mad not. You with joking."

She studied his face then nodded. "Okay Yoda."

He growled again, but made sure he didn't look mad.

She gave him an ornery grin that made her eyes sparkle despite the blue contacts. "Let's run." Abruptly there was a white wolf at his feet.

Grinning himself, he popped into his own wolf form and joined her.

DAMIEN – NOVEMBER 25 – WITCH'S HOUSE

"Damn," Hilda said, after tapping her phone off.

"What?" Damien asked.

"It was her. It was definitely her. They had the house surrounded. She and the boy got away."

"How?"

The witch slammed her fist down on the old metal desk in the basement. "I don't know. They didn't detect a portal and they had a blocking spell in place."

"Maybe she ran."

"Do you not know what surrounded means? The owner of the house said they'd gone back to the bedroom to put on their shoes, but no one saw them leave by any of the windows."

"Brayton was okay then?"

Hilda shot him a sharp look. "Concerned for your traitorous friend?"

"He's not traitorous, just loyal to the wrong person, and yes. He's been through a lot." It was too bad Honey was a hybrid. She was pretty and strong and although she was too young for *him*, she and Brayton would have been a nice couple. He had to admire Brayton's stubbornness when it came to her even if it couldn't go anywhere.

The witch shrugged. "I didn't ask about Brayton. He was well enough to walk."

"What do we do now?"

"Brayton is going to need medical attention. No one has ever gone that many rounds with the extractor without having their brain scrambled. He's going to be more of a hindrance than a help." She tapped the ugly looking crown-thing with a chuckle. "I'll bet she runs to her grandmother. If she does, my people will be waiting."

"Will she be able to help him?"

"Rachel? Maybe. I'm actually surprised she was able to do so much after that fire. I couldn't tell he'd been burned at all. The way Lynn went on about it, he was crippled and horribly disfigured for life."

"He lost an eye," Damien reminded her.

"Couldn't tell."

"What if Honey doesn't take him to Mrs. Wixx? Will he be okay?"

"No idea."

"His parents are going to be looking for him. If he tells them what we did, the Enforcers will be after us."

"Then I guess you better find him and the girl first."

"How am I supposed to do that? The whole world has been looking for Honey for months and every time anyone gets close, she vanishes."

"She has other friends. We could set a trap. When she comes to rescue them, we'll have her, and everyone will overlook what had to be done to get her. It's either that or vanish yourself and let your brother have your pack."

Or he could tell Alpha Brandon what happened and plead his case. Alpha Brandon was soft. He might not even have him arrested. If he didn't go to jail though, his dad would likely relegate him to mopping floors in the brewery for the rest of his life. Deacon would still get the pack and he'd still be without his power. The only possible good that would come of it was taking Hilda down with him. On the other hand, if he did capture Honey, he'd be a hero. She probably wouldn't remove the binding spell on him since she'd be mad at him, but if he was a hero, surely another witch would help. He'd insist one of them remove the spell before turning her over. Hold on. Maybe he could free her in return for having the spell removed AND having Brayton's promise not to persecute. That would be perfect.

"They'll have WOLF in the morning but there will be too many witnesses to pick them up then. I can probably pick them off one-by-one after that. You got more of that sleeping powder?"

"I do."

"No torture this time though. She's moved on. They won't know where she went."

"They might know her plans though."

"We already know her plans. She's trying to break the curse."

"But how far has she made it? Does she know where the other pieces are? If so, we could lay traps there too."

"I mean it. No torture. I don't care if you use a spell on them to force them to talk, just no torture."

"Bring your brother then."

"What?"

"He can force them to talk with all that alpha power he's stolen."

"No. He can't be a part of this. If he finds out why I'm doing this, he'll stop me."

"So don't tell him."

"He'll know."

77

"Then find somebody else. I'm not picky. It's either that or torture."

17

HONEY – NOVEMBER 25 – WALLERAWANG, AUSTRALIA

"Why is everything so expensive?" Honey mumbled under her breath. The cheapest way to Melbourne she'd found so far was about $50, but that was by plane which she and Brayton couldn't use since he didn't have an ID with him and she was hiding from cameras. Melbourne wasn't absolutely necessary, but if she was going to find a witch library with information on retrieving things lost in the water in Australia, that's where it would be. Also, there might be someone there who sold portals.

"Wrong what?" Brayton asked sleepily. He'd put his head down on his arms as soon as they'd sat down at one of the well-used library terminals in the human library.

She reached over and rubbed Brayton's broad shoulders through Jay's pullover. "Nothing."

He'd impressed her. He'd run over twenty-five miles without complaint, then followed her around while she bought ingredients and made him an anti-finding/protection hairband, and that was all before they'd sat in the library for a couple of hours. She did one last search, then deleted her browsing history and closed her incognito window.

Collecting the pictures and maps she'd printed off, she stood and tapped his shoulder. "Come on, let's send the letter, get some supplies, then we'll go camping."

He lifted his head from his arms. "Sausage dogs?"

"Sure, we can make some."

He looked like a growing tree in a time-lapse film the way he slowly stood, then put his arms out to stretch. She controlled the odd urge to touch him by reaching up and adjusting the bucket hat she'd found for him that didn't match at all with the sweater-like pullover he was wearing.

"Ridiculous I look."

"Who are you trying to impress? Me?" She waved at the well-used cowboy hat, over-sized pink-framed ombré tinted sunglasses, and itchy long, brown wig she'd braided down her back over the plaid farmer's shirt she'd found at a thrift store in Sydney. The faded jeans that completed the outfit didn't quite disguise her lack of boots.

"Good look you."

"We'll buy you more clothes – a couple of T-shirts and shorts at least."

"Underwear?" he asked, tugging on the seat of his pants.

"Yes, definitely, and a toothbrush."

He breathed into his hand and made a face.

"Come on."

She didn't manage a single step before his warm hand slipped into hers. It was both sweet and concerning since she was pretty sure his need to be close to her was due to whatever trauma Damien and the witch had subjected him to. He had even said the 'L' word when he called her for help. He couldn't have meant it. They were both too young for something like that even if he thought they were fated mates.

Were they? She did like kissing him.

Later. She could think about this later – much later.

80

She led him behind the library where the sign pointed for the public toilets.

"Here, you hold these," she handed him the papers she'd printed out in the library, "and I'll send the letter."

"Should go I you with."

"That would not be quiet. Here," she pulled out her last portal and offered it to him. "If I'm gone longer than I should be, you can use this to get home."

"I you go with," he insisted stubbornly, putting his hands behind his back so she couldn't hand it to him.

"Brayton, I need to use the bathroom. You're just going to have to wait here, okay?"

"Letter the?"

"Was your idea. The pop-in pop-out was your idea."

"Idea bad."

"Well, I guess we don't have to send it," she conceded, tucking it back into her pocket, "but I still have to use the bathroom."

He nodded, looking for all the world like a little boy who didn't want to lose sight of his parent. She squeezed his hand. "I'll be right back."

Walter didn't even notice her sudden appearance in his room. She left the note on top of his charging cell phone and popped right back out. Just in case, she paused for a moment in the nether to make sure no spy spells had hitched a ride, then popped back into the bathroom.

"There Honey in you are?"

If Brayton pounded any harder he was going to break down the door.

"Yes. I'm not done yet. Stop hitting the door."

"Minutes over five it's been!"

"I'm a girl."

"Honey." Something heavy thumped against the door.

"A few more minutes. I promise. I was delivering the letter."

"Know I."

Bladder empty and hands clean, she opened the door, ready for a full-on hug. Instead, Brayton lifted his tear-streaked face from where he'd clearly had his head against the door and gave her the most mournful look she'd ever seen. A strange, almost overwhelming feeling filled her chest and she simultaneously wanted to embrace him and punch the people who'd hurt him.

"Can't live this I like."

She wrapped him in her arms, and gently led him away from the bathroom door in case someone came by. They were lucky no one had been around to witness Brayton's mini-meltdown.

"You don't have to. You're just suffering the after-effects of whatever they did to you and I think you've moved beyond tired. You just need a few days to recover," she hoped.

"Lose to you want don't I."

"I don't want to lose you either," she said honestly.

He sighed and leaned into their hug so heavily, she had to shift her stance to provide enough support to hold him up.

"No problems with the letter," she pushed out cheerily against his shoulder. "Walter didn't even stir. I paused for a little in the nether to make sure no spy spells followed me. That's probably what took so long. I think time goes by faster there. I'm sorry I'm worried you."

He sighed.

"Brayton, you're heavy." She pushed him upright.

"Let's go to the store and get you some cooler clothes, then you can nap while I get a campfire started."

He was upright, but he looked saggy, like a sad Woody doll. They were never going to make it through a store. So be it.

"Come on, just a few more blocks, and you can sleep."

18

BRAYTON – NOVEMBER 26 – WALLERAWANG

Brayton closed his eyes again. He hoped Honey had a plan that did not involve any more camping in the Australian outback. Crickets or whatever bugs those were, he could handle, but the other sounds the Australian animals made were something else. His eyes flew open. That wasn't an animal, not one with paws currently, anyway. He stroked the top of Honey's head. In the dark of the tent, her white fur glowed on its own. Only in his fondest dreams had he ever imagined sleeping next to her like this – as friends with the promise of something more. She still didn't seem as gone on him as he was on her, but she was letting him kiss her. That was promising. Her eyelids slid open and she gazed up at him sleepily from beside the pillow.

"Is something wrong?" she sent telepathically.

He touched his ear to indicate she should listen and his nose to signal her to smell.

She sniffed. *"Wolves. They're probably camping too."*

He shook his head. He couldn't understand what they were saying, but he was very certain there were several and they had the tent surrounded. As if they'd realized he was on to them, a knife pierced the fabric on the side of the tent and sliced down.

"Jerks!"

He felt rather than saw Honey transform. The knife stopped moving and he was pretty certain she'd froze the owner of the knife, although he didn't smell her magic. The tent was too small to stand or to do much other than sleep, but she had somehow scooted past him and was already unzipping the door.

"Wait!"

"It's not witches. They're Aboriginals, AND THEY HAD NO RIGHT TO CUT UP MY TENT!" she finished on a yell.

The three Luna marks on her head pulsed brightly. Wow. He'd seen her mad before, but never like this.

"There charge maybe shouldn't out you just."

Annnnddd, his mouth still wasn't working.

"Oh, I'm charging." She looked back at him. "You should charge with me."

Did that mean she had a plan already? He hoped.

Honey crawled out of the tent and put her hands on her hips to glare at the ten mostly naked men surrounding them. He was pretty certain she was glaring, at least. He couldn't see her face but a couple of the men were looking anywhere but at her.

"Who gave the order to destroy my tent?" Honey demanded, walking over to the man still frozen in the act. She pulled the knife out of his hand, then shoved him away. Since he caught himself when he fell, Brayton concluded Honey had thawed him mid-shove.

"That would be me, Luna," a taller man with skin so dark he would have been invisible in the night if it weren't for the white paint decorating his body from head to toe.

"Why?"

"Because you no longer need it since you will shortly

85

be my Luna."

"And what makes you think I'm going to be your Luna?"

"You are on my land and I will defeat your chosen one."

"This is a public park."

"Only for humans."

He sounded way too smug. Honey wasn't going to like that.

"If I defeat you, will that make this my land?"

"No. If your chosen one defeats me, which he won't, you can leave."

"He is not fighting for me. I fight for myself and since you cut up my tent, my property, my land, as it were, when I win, this campground becomes mine and all of you will be on my land, which means you'll be mine too."

Where was she going with this? She probably could beat the guy, but why would she want to claim ten men?

The black and white man laughed. "You will be fun to tame. Now stand down Luna, so we can get this done."

As Brayton had known would happen, the alpha tried to use his power on Honey. She went right through it. The alpha had the sense of mind to raise his staff, but it was too late. Honey swiped his feet out from under him and had him pinned with the knife at his...balls...okay.

"I win. You're mine. I don't want you so go home, and don't ever talk about taming a woman again or I will make these," she tapped his jewels with the flat side of the knife, "disappear".

She rolled off the man's legs and was back at Brayton's side before the alpha could gulp.

"Kill them!"

"Not today," Honey said calmly before Brayton had even worked up a good panic. Everyone stopped moving everything except their eyes. Freaky.

Honey sauntered back to the alpha whom she had frozen so that he was leaning back on his elbows. "You are a bully and a sore loser. For that, I take away your alpha power until the next full moon." She squatted down and touched his head. "The rest of you, feel free NOT to listen to him for the next couple of weeks. In fact, I command you not to listen to him at all when you're on my land." She threw the knife between the alpha's legs. Brayton winced at how close it came to what was certainly fragile skin. Honey didn't even look. She marched passed Brayton and made the tent vanish, then took his hand. "Let's go. We should run. They'll thaw in about thirty seconds."

"To where?"

"The bathrooms. We can portal from there. Melbourne can wait."

"Power did really take you his away?" he asked once they'd slowed down.

"No. I bound it, but only loosely. It will unravel eventually, hopefully by the next moon."

Her hand was trembling. His strong little Luna wasn't as hard as she portrayed. He gave her hand a gentle squeeze.

"You would I for fight."

"I know, but he was a jerk and I'm not property. Besides, I figured if I defeated a bunch of men, word would spread and the packs here would think twice about taking me on."

Despite her many male friends Honey was clueless

sometimes.

"Challenge or they it find a would."

"Oh. Good point."

How had she figured out that garbled mess so fast?

He wanted to tell her that men, himself in particular, didn't want to fight for her because she was property, he wanted to fight for her because she was something special and worth putting his life on the line for, but with the way his mouth was twisting things, he doubted even she could understand all that.

19

BRAYTON – NOVEMBER 25 – SOUTH AFRICA

"Are we where?" Brayton asked, looking around at the surprising variety of plants all around them.

Honey pulled a small round thing out of her pocket and turned slowly in a circle. "This way."

"Is that what?"

"A compass. I found it in Jay's things when I got you clothes."

"North point?"

"Yes, it still points north and the sun still sets in the west. We're about 8 hours behind Sydney here, which is why the sun is still up."

"Back went time we in?"

She grinned at him in the fading light. "Yep."

"Going are where we?"

"Somewhere here." She stopped and looked around again. "No one has posted a picture of this location online, but the coordinates are not far from the tree we popped out of. Do you smell any magic?"

He shook his head.

"I don't either."

A moment later she was a beautiful white wolf. Although he'd seen her do it several times now, it still amazed him how fast she could transform, and how fast he could do it now too, with clothes! He joined her in sniffing around the trees but even with his full wolf nose, he couldn't sense a thing.

"*This isn't working,*" she admitted after their third time around the area.

"*You said you felt the other one.*"

"*There were several powerful curses and an illusion spell with it and your words came out right! You're getting better.*"

"*Maybe feel and sit?*" he suggested.

"*You mean sit and feel?*"

"*That yes.*"

She sat down on the dark side of a large tree and closed her eyes. He tried to sit and feel for a tingle or anything that might be magic for a couple of minutes but decided to forgo that exercise when a red cricket-like insect with tusks crawled across his foot.

Where would a witch have hidden a thin piece of metal? There wasn't anything here but trees and plants. If it were him, he'd bury it far beneath a newly planted tree, something that would likely last a long time. He gazed up at the dark branches of the tree Honey had walked toward when they first arrived. That would work.

"*To tree nether send?*"

"*Why? Do you feel something?*"

"*No. Guessing.*"

"*Which one?*"

He nodded toward it.

"*That's big. I've never sent anything that big to the nether.*"

"*It matters does?*"

"*I don't know.*" She prowled around the base of the tree he'd indicated. "*Also, once the roots are gone, the dirt will cave in.*"

"*Not all.*"

She popped into human form abruptly. "Stand back. You can rescue me if I fall in."

"What? Wait!"

She touched a big root several feet from the tree.

The tree vanished.

She did not.

He huffed in relief.

"I need a flashlight." She picked up a stick and stabbed it into the ground in front of her foot. "So I touch it exactly right when I bring it back," she explained, then backed away and produced a tent – Jay's tent.

Brayton fought to control his jealousy while she unzipped the tent and reached in for a backpack.

"He brought all kinds of useful camping supplies. He even had a little pan," she held it up with a grin, then her face fell and she sighed and tucked it away. "Found it."

She waved something that did not look like a flashlight at him, then tucked the bag back into the tent and sent it to the nether again.

"Hand's free," she said, slipping something over her head, then grinning at him in the dark.

"You look…"

"Like a dork. I know," she said. "I teased him about it all the time. He liked to wear it when he was writing at night before we went to bed."

"Writing?" Brayton eked out while not growling at the 'we' before 'bed'.

"Yeah. He wrote poems. He wrote one about me. He called it 'Woman of Mystery'. I think he was trying to get me to talk about myself. It made me work harder not to."

Her teeth flashed with a smile in the dim light, but his nose caught a whiff guilt and grief.

"Read it I can?"

"I gave the notebook to his mom."

"Oh. Was it good any?"

"I liked it."

"Careful," he said when she approached the hole again. It had to be at least fifteen feet across. She waved her hand at him to shush him, then got right up on the edge before she flicked on her light.

"See what do you?"

"A hole. If someone did put the tablet under this tree, they either dug pretty deep, the tree pushed it down, or the roots engulfed it. I don't feel anything. I'll pop up into the nether and…"

Something dark moved on the wall on the opposite side of the hole, reflecting Honey's light just enough that Brayton noticed it. He didn't recognize it, but some part of him must have sensed it was trouble because his fight or flight response was definitely leaning toward flight. *"That's what?"*

She blinded him with her light. "Where?"

"The up side climbing hole the of."

"Where?" Her light zipped back to the hole. "Oh. Ants. Lots and lots of ants." She took a step back just as they surged over the edge of the hole.

"Come from where they did?"

"I don't know," she said, still backing. "Maybe moving the tree disturbed an anthill."

He'd never seen so many ants in his life. They were like lava boiling out of the ground.

"Do ants bite?" She swiped at something on her ankle. "Ow. Yes, they do. Run Brayton, back to the tree we portalled to."

The tree wasn't far, and the ants were fast, but not that fast. Honey arrived right after him. She jabbed her elbow against the tree, then threw her arms around his wolf.

"Hold your breath."

20

HONEY – NOVEMBER 25 – NETHER

Honey jumped and nearly screamed at the smooth face with blank eyes and an open mouth bobbing in the nether under the light of her head lamp. A mermaid? Why would anyone send a carving of a mermaid into the nether? She kicked away, dragging Brayton with her. The carving followed, or it seemed to in the light. In fact, everywhere she turned, objects were crowding in on them. Had they done that every time or did it just seem that way because she could see them now? She needed to breath. She focused on one of her tethers and pushed.

"Cave Sydney near?" Brayton asked telepathically.

Honey turned in a circle to scan the rock walls with her head light. No eyes or faces looked back. "Yes," Honey said, letting out a deep shuddering breath.

"Okay?"

How was Brayton so calm?

"Did you see them?"

"What?"

"All the things coming toward us?"

"Things?"

"Yeah, the mermaid and the trunk and the other stuff floating in the nether."

"Nothing toward come us."

"It looked like it."

Brayton popped into his human self and pulled her

into his arms just as her whole body started to tremble.

"Hey. Okay it's," Brayton said against her hair, then sighed.

She needed to figure out how to fix him, but for now...she leaned into his hug, savoring the contact with another person, with Brayton. It took a few minutes, but her body did eventually stop trembling.

"Okay?" Brayton asked.

She nodded but didn't move from his shoulder and he didn't loosen his grip.

"Now what?" he asked against the top of her head.

"I have to put the tree back before it suffocates in the nether."

"Magic ants?" he asked.

"I don't know. I've never disturbed an anthill before," she shuddered.

"Weakness found," Brayton said.

She pushed away from him with a scowl. "I am not weak!"

He opened his mouth like he wanted to say something comforting, then smirked instead.

She shoved at his chest. "Stop it!"

"Maybe. Not. Right. Tree," he said carefully.

"I still need to put it back."

"Inspect. First. Here."

"There's no room for the roots."

"Water," he pointed toward the cave entrance.

There was a river down the hill from the cave that might be deep and wide enough. It wasn't a bad idea. She nodded.

"I. First," Brayton said and popped back into his wolf form.

Also not a bad idea since who knew what wolves or dingoes might be roaming close by and his nose worked better then hers. She switched off her headlight and waited in the mouth of the cave until he telepathically told her it was safe, then followed his pale form between the boulders and down the slope.

"I can't tell if it's deep enough," she commented, looking out over the dark water.

Brayton jumped in. His wolf head went underwater, then popped back up as human. "Deep. Here." He moved closer until his naked shoulders started to appear. "Not."

"Where are your clothes?"

He grinned. "Not. Wet."

"I don't think I've ever transformed without my clothes. Impressive."

He gave firm nod, then stretched out his hand. "Come."

"Um, you come out first."

Instead of teasing her about her adversity to being naked in front of people, he gave her another little nod, then popped back into his wolf form and swam ashore.

If Brayton could transform sans clothes after only having the ability for a mere week-and-a-half, she should be able to do it too. She transformed into her wolf form and leaped like he had, then popped back into her human form sans clothes once she was submerged.

"The water is freezing. Why didn't you warn me?" She grumped at him.

He laughed in her mind from where he was sitting on the shore in his nice fur wolf coat.

"Rude." With her less-than perfect swimming technique, it took her longer than it had Brayton to get close enough to shore to touch the bottom. By the time she was walking, he was pacing the edge of the water like he was about to jump in.

"I'm fine."

"Can't swim you?"

"I'm not a fish like you, if that's what you mean. Get back. I'm going to try and place the tree so it's laying toward the shore with its roots in the deeper water."

She put her hand out over the water. The tree popped out laying down right where she imagined it, surprising her. Maybe she had more control than she realized.

Using the trunk, she started pulling herself back toward the deeper water around the roots of the tree.

"Still not feeling anything."

"Careful."

There was that BB she knew and well, not *loved*, but would be fun to tease. She made a squeaking sound like something had grabbed her foot, while simultaneously pushing herself under. To make it extra dramatic, she threw her hands above the water as her head went underwater.

"Honey!"

There was a splash behind her. Uh oh. She pulled the under-layer of clothes she'd been wearing from the nether just before a hand yanked her up.

"Honey! Okay?"

The whites of Brayton's eyes glowed in the faint starlight. He truly looked scared. Maybe she'd gone too far.

"I'm fine."

He studied her face, then pushed her toward the tree. "Me trick?"

97

"Me?" she asked innocently. She managed not to smile but couldn't prevent her lips from twitching.

"You," he said with a growl in his tone, crowding her up against a wide root.

She was pretty sure he was going to kiss her again, and even tilted her head up to make it easier, but he shifted his head to the side at the last moment and kissed her cheek.

"Two play can," he whispered in her ear.

She shrugged and spun in the water, putting her back to him so she could continue what she'd been doing.

She could feel him watching her. Barely three seconds later, she was spinning back around and his lips were against hers. It was a good kiss, one Blaze, her blue-haired witch friend would call a toe-curler.

Brayton finally pulled away and put his forehead against hers. "Drive you me crazy."

"I thought you were already there."

He growled at her and kissed her again. Other than his lips, he didn't touch her, but she could feel the heat of his body warming the chill of the cold water between them. She'd been in contact or near contact with his skin plenty of times during practice, but she'd never yearned to get closer to him like she did now. Then again, she hadn't been floating in freezing cold water either.

She pushed him away and tapped the cheek under his magic eye. "See anything?"

He scowled at the tree behind her. "No."

"Why don't you look on the other side and I'll search on this one. If it's here, I bet the tree grew around it and it's stuck in the middle of the roots or something."

He sighed, but then sunk down under the water to cross below the trunk to the other side.

She didn't see anything or feel anything but something, maybe the ants she'd have to face to put the tree back, pushed her to be as thorough as possible.

"Anything?" she asked when Brayton swam up to her again.

He shook his head.

"Guess we ought to put it back then."

"Seek?"

"I don't have a map of the tree."

"Tree have you."

"It doesn't work that way. The seeking spells are on the maps. Users just supply the clue and the activation word."

"Try."

It wouldn't work, but she pulled the other tablet out of the nether anyway and tried saying the magic word while holding the tablet over the tree. The tablet, still wrapped in a scarf at the end of a string so no one in the library would see it for what it was, didn't move.

"See," Brayton said.

She offered it to him. Brayton sniffed it, then sniffed the tree. A moment later, he was a wolf, clawing his way into the roots.

"Here. Light."

She sent the tablet to the nether again and pulled out the headlamp instead. A dull scrap of metal was embedded in the trunk where Brayton indicated.

"More."

She moved the beam around to reveal jagged little pieces of metal twisted, torn apart, and partially engulfed by the roots. One of the larger pieces had scratches on it that may have been letters.

"Tree. Destroyed."

"I...I think you're right. That's why I couldn't sense anything. The magic is gone."

Hot tears blocked her vision although she wasn't quite sure why. Relief? Just two more to go. Brayton transformed, then put an arm around her and pulled her to his side. Somehow his skin was still warm despite the chill in the water.

"Go. Now?"

"Yes. Hold your breath. I'll pull the tree up to us in the nether so I don't mess up the anchor I already have on it."

She felt him nod, then felt his warm lips against her cold cheek just before she sent the both of them to the nether again.

If things came at her in the nether, she couldn't tell with her eyes closed. Back on the ground, she quickly scanned the ground. but although there were still a few ants mingling around, they weren't surging anymore. She tiptoed past the creatures to her stick, which had thankfully withstood the surge, and pulled the tree out of the nether while willing it to snap back in place exactly how it had been. She assumed it worked since it didn't fall on her, although *she* felt like falling. Brayton, back in wolf form again – he must really like being able to transform so fast – put his head under her hand.

"Come. Sleep. Watch I."

They *had* missed out on several hours of sleep thanks to those stupid Australian wolves. She nodded and followed him down the brick path, well away from any remaining ants, until they found a nice bush to curl up under in their wolf forms and fall asleep.

21

HONEY - NOVEMBER 26 - SOUTH AFRICA

Despite the gentle yet steady rain, it was relatively dry under the broad-leaf plant they'd slept under. Not completely dry though. Honey shook her head to clear the water droplets from the end of her nose.

"Next what's?" Brayton asked. His warm nose rested over her shoulders and his side pressed against hers. It was nice. He really seemed to like her, but…it was Brayton.

"We need to find a healer for you. I think we're six hours ahead of Indiana, so it should still be dark there. We can check the slate and see if Walter got my hint about giving it to your dad or we can just drop in on…Walter," she finished over her growling stomach.

He nudged the back of her head with his nose. *"First eat."*

"We'll need to be human."

The sparse clothes she'd been wearing during their swim were still going to be wet, but since it was raining… She stuck her head out from under the leaves and looked up and down the foliage-line path. No one was in sight. She crawled out from under the bush and transformed beside the trunk of a wide tree. Even with her human height, she still couldn't see anyone.

She gestured to Brayton, "Come on. We can pretend we're jogging tourists looking for a good place for breakfast."

"Dog a be I'll."

"You're too wolfy to be a dog."

"Wolf-dog."

She could understand his reluctance to go human again. Jay's clothes were made for cooler weather and would be uncomfortable to run in.

"Okay, but you'll need a leash. They probably have leash-laws here."

She pulled her backpack from the Nether and whipped her emergency scarf out from the front pocket. She'd purchased the silky thing as a head scarf, but when she pulled it out of the bag, it turned out to be long like a neck scarf. That's why it was now her emergency scarf, but it would also make a pretty leash.

Brayton eyed it doubtfully. *"Leash a that's not."*

"It's all I have. Besides, it will make you look less scary."

"Does it?" He curled the skin back away from his teeth to show off his impressive canines while she secured the scarf around his damp neck.

She whacked the top of his long nose. "Stop that." Then, because he was allowing her to tie a scarf around his neck, and it did look sweet even with his wet fur, she kissed the tip of his nose. "Behave and I'll find us bacon."

"Bacon like you?"

She picked up the free end of the scarf and started jogging. "I don't know if it likes me, but I like it."

He snorted and combined with the bow she'd fashioned around his neck, it made her laugh.

She'd been afraid that it was too early for them to legally be in the garden, but not one of the few people wandering on the well-tended paths appeared offended by their presence and the gate to the garden was open. They crossed the parking lot and popped out onto a two-lane road with a narrow sidewalk on one side.

"Which way you think?"

Brayton sniffed the air and turned left.

The few articles and videos she'd seen about Africans had always shown them living in arid regions with houses made of scraps, but this town looked a lot like any other town she'd been to, except cars were going the wrong way on the roads, and there were palm trees. On second thought, she commented to herself when Brayton tugged her down a one-lane alley, there were a lot of fences. She couldn't see any breaks in the sturdy stone and metal fences on both sides of the road, but maybe that was just this neighborhood.

They turned onto a four-lane street with wide sidewalks on either side. The long, low row of buildings along the sidewalk on their side of the street either set behind a fence or had a front that made up part of the fence. According to her nose, at least one of them was open for breakfast.

"Good choice. Oh. Stop for a moment. I have an idea."

He obediently sat down and pretended to pant while she crouched down by his side and discretely pulled her doggy backpack from the nether.

"You can wear this, then I'll be able to change if they don't allow wet people in running clothes."

He looked at the pack then at her like she was asking him to put on a ballet skirt or something. *"Really?"*

"You've never worn one of these? They're really

useful. Plus it has a loop for a leash, so I can give you more room."

"Fine."

He obligingly stood still so she could snap it on him, but he made no effort at all to make it easier. She transferred her scarf to the leash loop then stood back to survey him.

"Now you look like a well-tamed dog ready for any adventure."

"Great."

"You're getting hangry, aren't you?" She knelt down and rubbed the fur behind his ears in a way she personally knew was irritating, "my adorable little fluffy bunny."

He gave her a look that would have scared people who didn't know he was human. *"It pushing."* He added a growl under his breath, but she suspected it was because of his difficulty with words rather than because he was truly mad.

She kissed the center of his forehead. "Come on."

The food was delicious and they accepted her cash card. The only issue was the disgusted look the owner gave Honey when she said some of it was for her dog. Honey quickly made up a story about her dog getting injured because he was protecting her and it was her way of saying thank you. That seemed to appease the woman somewhat.

"Okay," Honey said, standing from where she'd been sitting on the curb next to Brayton to eat her food, "Do you want to transform or just go?"

"Go."

"Let's walk back to that alley. There's no way I can run after eating all that."

"Good."

She wasn't sure if he was commenting on the food or that she couldn't run or that he didn't want to run either.

The alley was devoid of anything to hide behind, but there were no people and no windows either if you stood close to the wall. She pulled out her backpack and checked the guys' slate. Nothing. Imagining Walter was probably sleeping on his back and all sprawled out like he normally slept, she stuck out the finger with her anchor to him so that it was at approximately bed height.

"Hold your breath."

22

DAMIEN – NOVEMBER 26 – WITCH'S HOUSE

"We can't keep them here forever," Damien argued, again.

"If you'd brought your friend, we wouldn't have to."

"I told you he was in an accident on the way here. His truck was totaled."

The witch dismissed his excuse with a wave of her hand and a roll of her eyes. "You're wolves. I'm sure he walked away. These four are staying here until we either get answers or capture the girl. I'm going to bed. They better be here when I get up or I'll make sure you take the blame for everything."

"You're going to blame me for breaking the spell on that ugly crown? I don't see that sticking."

The woman's lips went narrow with anger. "Stupid girl. I can't believe she threw it. It was a priceless level three artifact. The Curator is going to have my hide."

"You were torturing her friend. She probably didn't care what it was."

Hilda grunted and stomped up the stairs, leaving him with the four Little boys who were all chained together in a circle under the bright light. All four were slumped over and bloody from the beating he'd been forced to give them to keep blood-thirsty Hilda from cutting out their eyes. Not a single one had provided any useful information. He'd knocked them out mostly so he wouldn't have to hit them anymore. It was no fun pulverizing someone who couldn't fight back.

The tall one, whose glasses Damien had removed so they wouldn't get in the way, or so he'd told Hilda, raised his head. His long, narrow nose was swollen where Damien had accidentally broken it.

"What does that witch have over you Damien?"

"Nothing."

"Then why are you doing this?"

"I just need to speak to Honey. I want her to remove the binding on me."

"Then you're *not* going to turn her over to the witch?"

Damien looked up the stairs. The witch was gone, but he'd seen enough to know she had spells all over the room recording every sound and motion.

"I don't have to turn her over." He nodded to the white circle drawn around the boys. "You're inside an entrapment spell. If she comes here to rescue you, she'll be stuck."

"Why were you able to go in and out?"

"It's tuned to her blood."

"She's not going to come to our rescue. She has no way of knowing that we're in trouble."

"I know that, but Hilda thinks she will and until I can convince her it's not happening, you're staying there."

The blond lifted his head. His good-looking face was a mess. He'd likely heal right back to normal though, except for that deep scar Brayton's ring had left on his cheek.

"I don't believe you Damien," he said through swollen lips. "No alpha worth his salt would obey a witch the way you are. It's no wonder your powers are gone. You don't

107

deserve them."

Little twerp was trying to make him angry. The boy probably hoped it would get them free somehow which was stupid since there were tied up and beaten.

"You know, they will eventually figure out where we are and what happened to us," Zavier's beta tried again. "Zavier will know and he will prosecute. He won't care that you caught her or turned her in, in fact it will only make him more determined."

"Zavier," Damien snorted. It was ridiculous that his cousin had his own pack even if it was composed of only women and children and the skinny young man before him. "He'll be lucky if he keeps his pack. He knew she was a hybrid and didn't say anything."

"He didn't know," the boy insisted. "He knew she was different, just not why."

"Did you know?"

The boy gave a half-smile, probably all he could manage. "I knew she was different the moment I met her. All you have to do is look into those eyes of hers. She's so alive."

"And you seek to have her killed," the blond boy spoke, "just so you can have your stupid power back and lord it over all the other wolves. Is it really worth it to snuff out her life just for that?"

"I don't want her killed. She's a hybrid. I can't help that. Look," he glanced toward the stairs again. "I'll get you guys out of here as soon as she's captured. I truly didn't want to hurt you, but it was either that or the witch's knives. She's ruthless. You should have seen what she did to Brayton."

"What did the witch do to Brayton?" the smallest boy

asked. One of his eyes was swollen completely shut and all the skin around it was already a nasty shade of purple/blue.

Damien waved at the crown still sitting on the desk. "She tortured him with that. You ask a question and it causes pain if you lie or don't answer. Brayton refused to answer. It caused him so much pain he passed out four times. Honey popped in and rescued him after the fourth time."

"And Honey broke it," the boy asked.

"Yes."

"She portalled to him?" the fourth boy, the one with dark skin, asked. His face didn't look bad at all, but Damien was certain his stomach wasn't feeling so good. "She was probably just coming to visit. You can portal to people you know."

"How often does she portal to visit you?" Damien asked.

The boy shook his head, then winced. "She hasn't."

"Why would she portal to Brayton then?"

"I don't know."

Damien caught a scent on the air over the blood. The boy did know or knew something. It wasn't quite the truth.

Damien picked up the knife the witch had conveniently left on the desk. Maybe they just needed a little more incentive. "You guys have been holding out on me."

"Or you didn't ask the right questions," Zavier's beta said calmly.

"What should I ask?"

The short one huffed. "Like we would tell you."

Which one should he cut first and where? Should he cut off something or just slice? He didn't want to damage them permanently but a witch could probably replace small body parts.

"Look guys, I don't want to start slicing and dicing, but I need to find her. What is the relationship between Honey and Brayton?"

"Um, well," the blond began.

"See, even you know you didn't win that bet. Kissing is not getting together!" the short one proclaimed gleefully.

"They were kissing?" Damien asked at the same time the dark-skinned boy asked, "They kissed?"

"Ooo, boy and it was some kiss. I would've fanned myself if I had a fan," the short one said.

"Only old ladies and men who like men fan themselves," the blond dissed.

"Only lips were involved, but it would have definitely earned an R-rating," the tall one concurred.

"They're a couple." Damien summed. That would explain why Brayton was so stubborn about her.

"Yeah, who knows with Honey. Maybe kissing gives her some mystical, magical connection with a person. That could explain how she knew he was in trouble," the short one said. "I, unfortunately, have not experienced a kiss like that from Honey, so she won't be able to sense my predicament."

"Or mine," the tall one said.

"Or mine," the blond added.

"Or mine," the dark one said. The stench of anger coming off of him had increased at least ten-fold. Apparently, Brayton wasn't the only one with a crush on

110

Honey.

"Just let us go," the tall one urged, "and we won't tell anyone."

"Except Honey so she knows you aren't all bad," the little one said.

Their promises reeked of truth. "You'll ask her to help me?"

"Yes," the tall one said.

"And call me if you see her?"

"Our phones are monitored. We can't call you. If Honey wants to help you, she'll figure out a way."

"That's not good enough."

"Get us a couple of portals then. She can portal to you and back as soon as we give them to her," the little one said.

"Except you'll probably be watched so someone will be waiting to snatch her, or maybe you'll be waiting to snatch her yourself," the tall one said.

"I wouldn't do that. I don't care about the hybrid thing. I just want my power back."

"Then stop helping the witch. Prove you're not against Honey," the blond said.

"You don't think the witch won't find someone else, someone who doesn't care what body parts she chops off?"

Five eyes looked at him and the knife in his hand. The dark-skinned guy probably would have looked too, but he had a sore neck.

"I didn't cut anything off."

"You considered it," the blond said, "or you wouldn't be holding a knife."

"The witch didn't beat us either," the beta said. "I also

noticed you're at least twice her size. If she doesn't have a hold over you I can't help wondering why you let her boss you around."

"I think he's afraid of her magic," the little one said.

"What magic could she have that is so scary," the blond asked. "If she had anything painful or scary she would have used it on us."

The boys weren't dumb, he'd give them that. "That's not it. I need my power so I can take my pack back from my brother. I'm doing this for my pack."

"Is your brother a bad alpha?" the beta asked.

"That's not the point. I'm the eldest. *I'm* supposed to be alpha."

"Doesn't sound like you're doing this for your pack," the dark one said.

Abruptly, instead of four people inside the circle there were five and one wolf.

"Guys! What did he do to you?"

"Honey, we're inside an entrapment spell. We're bait," the little one warned.

The girl with the mostly shaved head didn't look at all like the Honey Damien remembered. Her ribs jutted out from under her running clothes and her face had lost any baby fat. She shot a click glance around the room so fast he wasn't sure she saw him, then she turned her attention back to the four in the circle.

"Oh, Walter, your nose, and Nathan, your cheek."

Damien watched as she touched and exclaimed over each one of them. Somehow, after she passed, their wrists and ankles were free, but the ties that bound them were still attached to the chairs. He would have tried to speak to her, but watch was all he *could* do.

"Can you guys walk?"

"I think so. Liam might need some help. Damien mostly got him in the stomach," the tall one answered.

Honey leaned over the nearly white wolf beside her and unclipped the pack from his back. "Brayton, why don't you transform and help him?"

That was Brayton? Damien didn't recall his fur being so light in color.

There was a pause, then she said, "But it will be easier if he can put his arm around you."

Another pause, then she said with amusement lacing her words, "You can't pull your clothes back, can you? I don't know why that would bother you. You didn't worry about clothes before."

There was a, not quite a flash, but abruptly Brayton was standing where the wolf had been in all his naked glory. Honey wasn't even looking. She was digging into the little bag she was now holding.

"I don't have anything here that will fit you. How about the scarf?"

She held a long, blue silky thing toward him while looking the other direction.

"No."

"Why? It will fit around your hips."

"No."

"Honey, we should hurry," the tall one interjected.

"Right."

She stepped right over the circle on the floor like it wasn't there and marched up to Damien. He wanted to ask again if she would remove the spell on him but he still couldn't move his mouth, and the three spots on her forehead shining like bright little stars distracted him.

"I am so angry at you. First, you steal Brayton's ring," she lifted his hand and nearly tore off his pinky while she was removing the ring. "Then you beat up my friends." She made a motion like she was pulling something out of the air. "I've removed the spell so you'll stop trying to pursue me, but you won't be able to anyway because you're going to jail, hopefully for a long time." She leaned closer to him and said in a low voice, "If you wake up and feel like you're floating, don't breathe."

23

HONEY – NOVEMBER 26 – INDIANA

"How are we getting out?" Luca asked after she'd sent a completely frozen Damien to the nether.

"Up the stairs and through the door."

"Where did you send Damien?" Liam asked.

"You guys didn't tell him?" She looked toward Walter who was helping Nathan up to his feet. Their faces made her want to cry.

Walter shook his head.

"Later then. I destroyed the spy spells that I could see around here and on you, but I suspect there are some I missed. Ready? We have to move quickly."

She ran up the stairs to the closed door. As she suspected, a locking spell held them in. She ripped it down, then did something she'd always wanted to try. She kicked the door. It slammed open, crashing into the wall beside it. Satisfying, but not enough to make up for what the witch had done to her friends.

The witch waiting on the other side squeaked, but determinedly uncovered the three freeze stones aimed at the door. Honey unfroze herself and ripped the spells from the stones. Freezing the woman didn't work. She was likely wearing a protective charm. Instead of breaking it, Honey pulled up a shield against any other spells to protect her friends coming through the door behind her, then wiped out the spy spells coating every surface of the room by sending out a second shield that rammed into them all.

The woman blew white powder at them. Honey stirred the wind and sent it right back into her face. It didn't appear to affect her either. She must have an antidote charm too, but the powder did make her take a step back.

"If you harm me it will just prove you're a monster."

Honey hesitated. There was another spell around her, something powerful – a protection spell but one with a kick.

"House," Brayton said.

She took her eyes from the woman and looked around. The stronger glow she could see around the woman did indeed extend to the walls of the house. She'd read about these – protection spells layered generation after generation on a building. They were considered level 4 spells due to the multiple makers, long life, and their ability to target multiple people. She didn't want to break it if she didn't have to. Truthfully, she wasn't sure she could.

"See if the house will let you leave."

"Without not you," Brayton said.

"I'll come to you. Hurry. I'm not sure how much time Damien has."

"What did you do to him?" the witch demanded. Spy spells were spilling from her hands like water.

Honey focused on the magic she could sense around the woman's neck and sliced at it with a sharp version of her shield spell. The woman didn't appear to notice it was down. The house must have though. The glow of magic pulsed and the door Walter had just opened in the kitchen slammed shut.

Phooey. "Step back close to me."

She waited for them to all be within touching distance, then, with her eyes still on the witch, crouched to touch the spell she could see on the house with her bare skin.

In her head she sent, *"House, I am not here to harm your owner. I only wish to rescue my friends whom she tortured. Look at them. They are all beaten and bloody. Please open your door and we will leave. They are innocent."*

With her magic sight, she saw spirals of different colors rising from the floor. "What are you doing?" the witch demanded.

Honey ignored her. The spirals started spinning around the room, some testing the shield over herself and her friends and some merely observing.

"Sorry about the door," she sent when a couple of spirals paused in front of it. *"It was locked and I didn't have the key. We're just trying to leave. I need to get them to the doctor."*

The spirals swirled together like they were communicating, then one of them broke off and dove into the witch's chest.

Her eyes rolled back into her head.

"What's going on?" Luca asked.

"There's a powerful protection spell on the house put in place by her ancestors. I asked them to let us leave. I think they are discussing it with her."

"Her ancestors?" Liam asked doubtfully.

"The essence of her ancestors," Honey corrected. "Whatever parts they put of themselves into the spells on the house."

The witch, whose eyes were still disturbingly white even in the dim streetlight coming in through the windows, spoke in a voice both hers and not hers. "You may all leave except the hybrid. She must stay and answer to her crimes."

"She has committed no crimes," Nathan spouted. "The witch lies."

"Do you wish to die for her, wolf?"

Honey stood. "They will go." She offered the keys she'd dug out of Damien's pocket and the ring still in her hand to Brayton, then placed a soft kiss on his lips to make sure her tether was still there and to remind him of it. "Let me know when you are completely clear of the property, at least a block away."

He curled his fingers around hers still in his palm. "Leave won't I you."

"I need you on the outside. Trust me."

"Honey."

She kissed his lips again and looked directly into his eyes, willing him to see that she had a plan and she needed them all safe in case she had to try plan B. "Trust me."

He gave a single, sad nod and pulled Liam's arm more securely around his shoulders.

"I am going to see them to the door," Honey announced to the house. "I will not attempt to leave that way."

"If you do, they will all die," the witch/other voice replied.

"I don't think I will be looking to purchase this house, ever," Luca commented from under Liam's other arm, "too bloodthirsty."

"And the wallpaper is sooo dated," Nathan said, while Walter helped him through the doorway from the living room to the kitchen.

"The kitchen isn't bad though," Walter said. "New flooring, counters, cabinets, and paint and it would be perfect."

To Honey's relief, the door out opened in front of him without his help. She hadn't been sure the house would keep its word.

"Skylight," Brayton added while waiting for Nathan and Walter to go down the few steps outside the door.

"Oh, yes. That would really brighten things up," Luca agreed. "Imagine if someone knocked out the little window above the sink and put in one of those windows you can grow plants in."

"A garden window," Liam wheezed.

"Yes, that," Luca agreed.

Brayton transformed back into his wolf form right before they stepped outside. Outside was pitch black except under the street lights. Honey guessed it was around 1 am. She watched from the door while they hobbled down the drive and to the street where she imagined Damien's truck was parked. It surprised her that the house let her stand so close to the door, but maybe it was hoping she'd try to leave. She stepped back once her friends were out of sight and shut the door herself.

"You will drop your shield," the house/witch demanded.

"Eventually. I'm waiting for them to get clear."

"You think you can take us on? Five generations have contributed to the protections on this house."

"I have no wish to take you on," but she would if she had to.

The walls glowed with colors that matched the different wisps. One of the ancestors clearly had conjuration powers since the door she'd busted was already back in place. She sensed enchantment, evocation, and illusion too. The living witch in front of her had some form of divination.

"Your family is very multi-talented." It wouldn't hurt to be polite while she was waiting for Brayton's all-clear.

"Flattery won't help you, murderess."

"I haven't murdered anyone."

"Everyone who dies because of the curse on you is your fault," the witch spit.

"No one has died because of any curse on me because there is no curse on me. I am a curse breaker."

"Lies," the witch/house screamed.

"You are only attempting to hold me here until someone can arrive to take me into custody, correct," she asked the witch.

"No. I have called the hunters. You will be shot on sight."

"Clear," Brayton's voice sounded in her head.

She dropped to a crouch to touch the floor. It would be difficult to bind the witch with the house protecting her, but she could bind the house. With a claw, she stabbed her finger and wiped the blood on the floor.

Imagining her blood soaking deep into the floor and forming a flowing ribbon that wrapped around the house, she said, "I bind the magic of this house and of all the people who claim relation to the previous owners of this house and who currently reside in this house, to this house. They cannot use or send their magic or anything they bespell past the boundaries of the walls that define this house as it currently stands."

She finished off the spell by tying the ribbon around the chimney. She thought about anchoring it to the nether, but figured her blood would cause enough problems. Plus, she was getting tired. Holding the shield up while the house was pounding on it was draining.

She stood slowly so that she only felt a little dizzy. "Good luck breaking that. Only another curse breaker can do it and if you keep killing the hybrids, there will never be another."

She sent herself to the nether before the witch/house could respond. A moment later, she was in the truck bed sitting over Brayton's legs with her lips on his. He jumped a little, then kissed her back gently, perfectly. After a minute or so, he pulled back, then put his forehead on hers with a sigh.

She rubbed his stubbly cheek. "Thanks for trusting me."

He shook his head. "Issue not trust. Want. To. Protect."

"I know, but you trusted I could handle it. Thank you."

He kissed her cheek, sending her butterflies fluttering again. The effect he had on her was so odd. Was it part of the fated thing? She pulled at the collar of the old T-shirt he was wearing. "You found clothes."

He curled his upper lip. "Damien's."

"Oh, yeah." She reached out into the empty space in the middle of the truck bed and pulled Damien from the nether. He was still frozen, just like she'd planned. In a frozen state she calculated she could tuck a person in the nether for at least 40 minutes Earth time before they woke up.

"Did you guys find any of those metal ties in his truck?" she asked.

"Yeah, there's a bag of them here," Luca pulled a

121

plastic bag with at least ten more zip ties out of the five-gallon bucket sitting behind the back of the cab.

"Any of those transformation blockers?"

"Mmm, nope," Luca said after stirring the contents around a few seconds.

"Brayton, can alpha commands keep wolves from shifting?"

"Yes."

"Will you?"

"Gladly."

She looked at the back of Walter's head in the driver's seat, and Liam slumped down in the passenger seat, and Nathan who was watching her through swollen eyes from the extended part of the cab and wished she could stay to make sure they were okay, but it was safer if no one knew she was around. She picked up an old, greasy bolt that was rolling around in the truck bed, touched the head to the inside of her wrist, then put it in Brayton's palm. "Anchor. Put this somewhere I can safely pop to anytime. I need to visit a water witch who might help us. I just have to convince her. Tell the guys what we know."

"You where are going?"

She kissed his cheek. "Where we suspected."

"Wait. What did you do to the wicked witch," Luca asked.

"Bound her powers to the house. No more spy spells, unless you feel like visiting her?"

Luca looked back in the direction of the house like he was seriously considering it then shook his head. "No."

24

BRAYTON - NOVEMBER 27 - INDIANA

"*Damien Meyer, eldest son of Alpha Mitchell Meyer of the Wolfborne pack, was arrested yesterday on multiple charges of kidnapping and torture after his five victims, all males and all sophomores at Vindale University, overpowered him and then drove themselves to the hospital with him in their custody. Mr. Meyer claims Ms. Hilda Brumsfield, a member of the advisory board at Vindale University, was the mastermind behind the crime and that he was only involved as a lie detector. The men, whose alphas requested we not reveal their identities, suffered lacerations, broken bones, internal injuries, and in one case, a magical injury to the brain. All are recovering and have been sent home. Ms. Brumsfield is wanted for questioning regarding the case but her whereabouts are currently unknown. The motive behind the kidnappings is speculated to have something to do with the elusive Honey Smith since...*"

"Brayton?"

Brayton tapped off the news report and closed his laptop. "Yes Mom?"

"How are you feeling?"

He spun in his desk chair to where she was poking her head past his door. "Fine." He blinked twice. No weird little creatures were sitting on his mother's shoulder or sticking out of her head. Whatever Honey had done to the witch was still working.

"Do you want to talk about it?"

"No."

She stepped inside and leaned back against the door frame with a sigh. "I'm sorry."

"For what?"

"I should have known something was wrong when I couldn't get a hold of you Saturday. Your father would have had people out sooner looking for you. You wouldn't have…you wouldn't have…" she started crying.

Brayton pushed out of his chair and rushed across the room to pull his mother into his arms. "Okay it's."

"No. It's not. I can't believe Hilda did this to you. I should have known not to trust a witch. This is my fault."

"No. Hers." He wanted so badly to say something longer than a couple of words, but for now, that wasn't possible. "Will. Get. Better."

"But you shouldn't have to get better," she wailed. "You should be having the time of your life in college, making new friends, going on dates, getting good grades, instead you lost an eye and got tortured. You haven't even been in contact with that…thing. I told Hilda that."

"Honey. Not. Thing."

His mother pushed back and put her finger nearly up his nose. "We do not speak that name in this house, Brayton Mooney."

"Lynn, do you mind if I borrow Brayton," Dad asked from the doorway, much to Brayton's relief.

"You're back! What did Damien say?"

"Nothing that he hasn't said before. Brayton, come see me in my office when you have a moment."

"Now. Good," Brayton said, stepping around his mother. He didn't even have to worry about her searching his things now since the slate was gone. Right, the bolt. He stepped back to his desk and picked it up.

"What's that?" Mom demanded.

He held it between his thumb and index finger. "Bolt."

"Why do you have that?"

Was his mom always this nosy? "Found."

She shook her head. "Men are strange."

Brayton tucked the bolt into his pocket so that the head was up, then followed Dad to his office. The task Honey had given him was turning out to be more difficult than he could have envisioned. He couldn't think of a single location to safely place a bolt where it wouldn't be disturbed and that was always clear of possible witnesses and that Honey would be able to leave from unnoticed.

His dad didn't say a word until he'd shut the door to his office and sat down at his desk. Then he pointed at the guest chair and said, "Sit."

Brayton obliged.

"Your grandpa and I went to question Damien along with Alpha Shane today. Did you know he got his powers back?"

"Yes."

"Do you know how?"

"Yes."

"Really?" Dad looked truly surprised. "Because he didn't seem to know. Even your grandpa couldn't alpha it out of him. In fact, every time we asked him who had overpowered him, he just said you got free but didn't know how. Somebody with alpha powers stronger than Grandpa's or a witch with a very strong spell got to him. Do you know who it was?"

"Yes."

"Who?"

Brayton pointed at himself. He hadn't realized his

power was so strong until Damien had tried to fight back with his own power. Defeating him had been like defeating a two-year-old at arm-wrestling.

"You?" His dad chuckled. "Your grandpa would have a cow. Who did it really? Only an established alpha with a Luna could be that strong."

He hadn't had a chance to have a good talk with his dad for a couple of weeks. How would he react to his news? Brayton grabbed the stack of post-it notes Dad always kept on his desk and a pen and wrote *"I have a Luna,"* then tore off the paper and stuck in on the desk in front of his dad.

His dad read the note, then looked blankly back up at him. "What?"

Brayton started writing, tearing off each little square as he finished and handing it to his dad. He told him about Jay and Honey and the aboriginals, although he just called them a pack. He then stood up and after wiggling his eyebrows at his father, transformed to his wolf and back in two blinks of an eye, complete with clothes.

Dad was literally speechless for several seconds.

"That's how Honey transforms, clothes and all?" he finally asked.

Brayton nodded, then wrote, *"That's why she never transforms in front of people. Also, you can see her Luna marks. They look like three diamonds across her forehead. All wolves can see them."*

"You can see them?"

Brayton nodded. *"And she can now speak telepathically, at least to me."*

His dad leaned forward and sniffed. "But you are still in my pack, although you do smell a little like her."

126

"I'm still pack because she chose me as her alpha and not the other way around."

"Use your power on me."

Brayton shook his head. He would never do that. "No."

His dad stood up. "Just make me sit down. That's an order," he said when Brayton shook his head again.

Since he insisted, Brayton focused his will on his dad and said, "Sit."

Dad's behind slammed into the chair so fast something cracked ominously in the chair.

"Wow."

Brayton shared a grin with his dad. They weren't power-hungry like the Meyers, but what red-blooded wolf wouldn't want to be strong?

"So, I guess this means I should consider Honey my daughter-in-law?"

Brayton rubbed his neck and looked away from his father's eyes. "No."

"No?"

He wrote, *"We've kissed but she's…not there."*

"And you are?"

"Yes."

"Mmm."

"Is. That. Okay?"

"You kissing her?"

Brayton shook his head and wrote, *"Having Honey as a daughter-in-law?"*

His dad read his note. Brayton couldn't read his expression when he looked up.

"Tell me something. Was she the reason you got loose?"

"*She rescued me Sunday evening,*" Brayton wrote. "*We were working on a way to get me safely here when Damien and the witch kidnapped her friends. She rescued them too and subdued Damien. She also took on the witch while we got out of the house. Honey bound the witch's powers to her house so she shouldn't be able to send more spy spells.*"

"She did all that? What did you do?"

"*Helped Liam out of the house.*"

Dad chuckled. "That girl. I couldn't think of a better mate for you, but your mother…"

"Know I," Brayton sighed.

"Where is your little Luna now?"

He shrugged.

"You think she's safe?"

"Hope."

"What did she think of your ailment?"

Brayton pointed to himself. "Yoda."

"She called you that?" his dad laughed. "I like it, Yoda."

"Dad!"

His dad sobered, "She couldn't fix it?"

"No."

"Guess she can't do everything." He stood and walked around the desk to pull Brayton up into a tight hug. "Glad you're safe son, and congratulations, you couldn't have chosen a better Luna to have your back."

"She. Chose. Me."

"Even better."

"Only. Option," he pointed out, only realistic one anyway.

"She'll get there. Why don't you get out of the house for a while, let your mom recover a little. I saw some of

128

the older kids heading for the trail with their bikes."

"Sure."

Maybe one of the bike sheds would be a good place to store the bolt. He pulled open the door to the one where his gear was stored and quickly shut it again, blocking out the sight of the two teenagers trying to swallow each other's tongues.

"Sorry."

Did he and Honey look like that? He wished. Would those two even notice if a girl popped into their midst? Better not risk it. What he needed was a barn or a shed where nobody went, but someplace Honey could easily travel from, or a way for her to travel from it. He eyed the shed where Honey's classic cycle that her father had given her was stored. That old human's barn where Honey's dad had stored the bikes would be perfect. He could even screw the bolt into a beam so it looked like it belonged there. All he had to do was convince the human who owned it to let him rent it without getting shot.

25

HONEY – THANKSGIVING – SYDNEY

Dear Pizza Thief (Nov. 26, 9 pm)

BB, huh? He's four years older than you. All home. 3 broken ribs but okay now. W's nose fixed. N almost pretty again. F kissed L to make it all better. Delilah jealous. Witch at large. D arrested. Alpha wants us to stay home until witch is caught. - L (the normal one.)

Dear BH (Nov. 27, 18:00)

Closer to 3. His birthday is at the end of June. I'm glad you are all okay. Say hi to F for me. Please let BB know you heard from me so he doesn't get anxious (stupid spell). - PT

Dear PT (Nov. 27, 9:22 pm)

BH? I know the H is for handsome, but what is the B for? BB says he loves Delilah, misses her, and planted a seed next to dad's surprise in the same soil. Seriously, what do you see in him? - HL

Dear BBH (Nov. 28, 14:30)

He never abandoned me. Happy Thanksgiving to you all. Tell BB thank you!

Honey tucked her magic slate into her backpack and

sent the whole thing to the nether. She hadn't had that long a conversation with Liam in forever. Maybe she shouldn't have called him Big Big Head, but he'd never know.

If she understood correctly, Brayton had found the perfect place for her bolt. It was currently the middle of the night in Indiana. That was both good and bad if she went there now. Good because if she went on the road with her bike, it would be harder to see her. Bad because she'd never driven at night and because Charlie was likely to shoot her if she woke him up. She could sleep there though. It would be more comfortable or at least quieter than the tent city she was currently in.

She unzipped the fly and crawled out of the tent. It was a good spot. Her tent was on the edge of the cluster of tents where it was easy to come and go. Even better, it was currently shaded by one of the tall buildings lining the road so the temperature was comfortable even though it was a warm day. She glanced around to see if anyone was watching. No one was, but oddly everyone she could see turned their head right before she made eye contact with them. Why were they afraid to catch her eye? Had the Enforcers or the hunters found her or was she being paranoid? She sniffed – everything smelled human. Maybe this spot had been empty for a reason. Had someone died here or something equally disturbing? She probably should have asked if it was okay to camp here before she set up her tent but it had been dark by the time she'd run from the cave and found herself some food. Then, she'd left super early this morning to stock up on groceries and check on Mr. Helman from afar.

It didn't matter. She'd be gone in a few minutes.

Despite all the camping she'd done, she didn't have much experience putting tents up or taking them down. Jay's tent, which she'd used since hers still had a hole, was more complicated than hers. She should have sent the silly thing to the nether this morning, but she didn't want to lose her spot in case she was staying another night.

The hairs on the back of her neck rose. Casually, she moved behind the tent so she could look over it and see what was coming. Three men approached in a triangular formation. The lead man's hair was shaved close, showing off a nasty scar on the side of his head. The other two had similar haircuts, just slightly longer. Her own hair was hidden under her winter beanie, odd for summer, but generally okay for a homeless person as long as she didn't have too many winter clothes on, which she didn't. Summer clothes made passing for a boy harder, but by hunching a little and wearing a tight running bra and an over-sized T-shirt, she thought she'd managed it.

The three planted themselves in front of her tent just as she finally finagled one pole end out of its grommet.

"Who are you?" the lead man asked.

"Leaving," she said in the deepest voice she could muster.

"You didn't pay for last night."

She looked around. The people who'd been chatting and sitting in front of their tents a few moments ago had all disappeared. That couldn't be good. She pulled the second pole out of its grommet while trying to decide how to answer. The tent collapsed.

"What for?"

"Rent."

She tugged at one of the poles. Instead of slipping out

132

easily, it got stuck inside the sheath that held it. Pretending to concentrate on it but still keeping an eye on the men who were spreading out to surround her, she said, "Are you the city?"

"Call us city workers. Pay up or we'll take it."

"How much?" She got the pole loose and quickly started folding it.

"Fifty," the head guy said.

She waved the folded pole at the surrounding tents. "No one here can afford to pay fifty for one night." She tossed the folded pole into the center of the tent, then squatted and started pulling out the other one.

"It's for one month."

"Then I owe you two dollars at most, except I don't believe I owe you at all."

"Last chance."

One of the quiet ones flicked open a knife.

"You'll have to wait until I finish with my tent."

"The price will only go up the longer you make us wait."

If anyone caught her using magic on humans, she'd be in big trouble, but hey, she was already in big trouble. She was ready to freeze all three of them if anyone moved but since they didn't encroach any farther, she held off. She hadn't smelled any magic, but it wasn't impossible that a homeless person could be a witch. If they witnessed her using magic on humans, they might report her. She folded up the last tent pole and tossed it into the center of the tent, then rolled it all up, ground canvas and all, like a big burrito. Now she just needed a piece of string, or a bag, or the nether. These guys couldn't have come at a worse time. From the ground, she scoped out her options. The

133

other tents were arranged in a sloppy grid pattern in the wide street between the tall buildings on either side. The three men stood between her and the closest sidewalk, but it shouldn't be hard run through the tents to the other side of the street.

She squeezed her tent burrito close to her chest and stood. "What's that?" She pointed past the speaker. The man holding the knife looked away. Good enough. She turned and ran.

The minute her back was to them, she sent the tent to the nether, but kept her arms close to her body until she was able to put a tent between them and bend a little like she was tossing her bundle somewhere.

She assumed the other tent people would not want to get involved, but, like mind-controlled zombies, they kept stepping into her path. Not all of them, just a few, but it was enough that she had to alter her course several times just to get to the other side of the street. Once there, she realized she'd been cut off in both directions by determined tent people. This couldn't be normal.

"Why?" she yelled at one woman who tried to hit her with an umbrella when she went by.

"Discount."

Darn it. There were no alleys, just a couple of dumpsters, so nowhere she could logically vanish from. The stores along the street were all closed.

There were only four men between her and the end of the street. If she could freeze their feet, she could get by. Something flew over her head and around her shoulders. Abruptly and painfully she was stopped in her tracks. A lasso? Really? She planted her feet and jerked on the rope, pulling the thrower closer to her instead of the other way around, so she could pull it off.

"What is wrong with you people?"

"You have to pay," the man said.

"Why?"

"Them's the rules."

"Where are they posted?" She was surrounded now, but only by the other tent people, not by the first three. They had slowed to a walk.

"Just pay and you can go," one woman said, looking over her shoulder nervously at the three approaching men.

"What if I don't have any money?"

The woman looked down at her feet, "They'll take other forms of payment."

"I'll bet. You guys did your jobs. Back up and let me talk to them."

Someone grabbed her elbow from behind. She jerked it away and spun toward the buildings so she'd have something solid at her back. Two other men and one woman had joined the first three who had approached her. The other people though, were all backing away with their heads down like they were bowing or didn't want to see what came next.

"If you won't pay in cash, we'll take a pound of flesh," the first man said, pulling out his own knife. Abruptly, they were all holding something sharp, including a large fork.

Fighting would cause a scene but freezing them and walking away would expose the witnesses to magic. She'd have to fight. She'd never taken on six people at once, but they were all human and she was good, even if she was out of practice.

"Before we get started, I feel I should warn you, I'm

135

really good at fighting – like award-winning."

"Sure you are," the leader said, "and I'm a Commando."

He was lying, but from the way he was holding his knife, he probably did have training of some kind.

What would the Black Widow do? Well, she probably wouldn't let them all converge on her the way they were. Channeling her speed, but not too much, Honey dropped down and swept the feet out from under the woman and the man next to her. She then sprang up and rapidly hit the nose, throat, and groin of the next man. By that time, the first guy to pull a knife was charging her with the knife. She blocked his arm and ducked just enough to get perfectly positioned to throw him over her body on top of the first two she'd knocked down. Knowing she didn't have much time before all three of them recovered, she turned to face the remaining two. The head guy had decided to join the fight, but he wasn't coming as fast as the first mad did. She squatted and got two punches into his solar plexis, a slice on her arm, a strong kick into his armpit, and then a left to the sweet spot on his jaw. He fell in front of the remaining man. Honey put her fists up. The last man wisely backed away. Not so wisely, the first guy she'd knocked down decided to try again. She rewarded him with a foot across his cheek followed by a fist basically up his nose. Noting the fork coming at her, Honey grabbed the woman's arm and flipped her over her shoulder onto the leader, then spun away so the lot of them were in a pile to her right and the wall was at her back again.

"Anyone else?"

No one would look her in the eye. "I'll consider you

satisfied then."

A superhero would probably walk away, but no way was she doing that, not with the sound of sirens and the cell phones that had appeared and had no doubt videoed the whole thing. She ran, ducked into the first alley she found, and vanished to the nether.

26

BRAYTON – THANKSGIVING – INDIANA

"Good Morning Brayton, Happy Thanksgiving."

Now what was his mother up to? She sounded entirely too cheerful.

"Brayton?" She frowned at him expectantly.

"Happy. Thanksgiving. Mom."

She smiled and nodded like he'd aced an exam. "Your grandparents just pulled up. Why don't you go out and welcome them."

At least half the pack was already welcoming them, but whatever. He went out and waited at the end of the sidewalk while his grandparents made their way across the drive past all the people who'd met them at their camper. Grandmother reached him first and pulled him into a hug.

"I'm so glad you're okay sweetheart."

"Me. Too."

His grandfather took a turn only after his wife was done. Brayton knew he was in trouble when he heard his grandfather take a sniff right next to his ear.

Grandpa pushed him away to hold him at arm's length and cocked his head. "Brayton?"

Brayton looked him straight in the eye. "Grandpa."

"We will have a chat."

"Yes. Sir."

Grandpa raised both bushy eyebrows. Brayton couldn't tell if he was impressed by his respect or thought

138

Brayton was trying to be cheeky.

"Brayton, Brayton, did you see this?" Malcolm asked out of nowhere, thrusting his phone under Brayton's nose.

"Happy Thanksgiving Alpha Braxton, Luna Nancy," Cici said politely behind Malcolm.

"Yes, Happy Thanksgiving," Malcolm threw over his shoulder, then shook his phone in Brayton's face, "Watch."

All Brayton saw were several people with their backs to him converging on something he couldn't see in front of a tall building.

"What?"

Malcolm shook the phone again. "Watch!"

All the people started falling down.

"You think it's real?" Malcolm asked. "It happens so fast. It could have been staged, but they don't look like they're acting."

A skinny kid in an overly large shirt with a knit cap pulled down over their ears and their fists raised stepped away from the pile of people, yelled something, then ran. The camera followed the kid until she or he disappeared around a corner. The shot was grainy like it had been zoomed in as far as it would go, but he was pretty sure it was Honey.

"What are you watching?" Grandpa asked.

Malcolm moved the phone from Brayton's face and handed it to Grandpa.

"Where?" Brayton asked Cici.

"Australia, yesterday afternoon. There are some other videos but that one is the best. Doesn't it look like..."

"Yes," he cut her off. "Happen why?"

"Something about a homeless turf war."

139

"Pretty good for a druggie," his grandfather said.

"Druggie?" Brayton couldn't help saying. "Because just…," he was going to stop himself there.

"Look how skinny he is and he doesn't even seem to notice the blood running down his arm. Probably high as a kite. I bet he stole money from those people to pay his habit."

"Other. Way. Round," Brayton ground out.

"You think they were trying to steal money from him?" his grandfather asked.

Brayton nodded.

"Shouldn't have run away from home then, should he?"

Brayton forced himself to unclench his fists. Punching his grandfather wouldn't do anyone any good, particularly him.

"Here dear, I made your favorite." Grandma pushed a box of something into his hands. He took a whiff. Gingerbread and pumpkin trifle, one of his favorite desserts, and one only his grandmother ever made and that wasn't very often.

"Best. Grandmother. Ever."

Malcolm made a face. "I don't know how you can eat that."

"More for us then, right dear," his grandmother said, linking her arm through Brayton's.

"Right."

Would Honey like it? Had she gotten his message? Was she even now on her cycle heading towards Texas? Not being able to communicate with her directly was driving him insane and it had only been a few days. Wait, what if she was on the cycle? She might be within range.

Maybe he could talk to her!

He forced himself to walk into the house at his grandmother's pace and hang about politely while his grandparents greeted his parents, but as soon as he could, he slipped away to his room and transformed.

"Honey? Are. You. Close?"

She didn't answer, but if she was on the motorcycle, she wouldn't be able to, not until she pulled off somewhere and found a place to transform.

"When. Chance. Respond. Please."

"Brayton, are you in here? Your grandfather is looking for you," his mom said, then opened the door and walked in on him.

Again, he was loving his new ability to transform instantaneously. He picked up his cell phone from the bedside table and shook it at her so she'd think he'd just come to get it.

"You know your grandfather doesn't like it when you pay more attention to that than to him."

"Looking. Something. Up."

"Well okay, but hurry. You know he doesn't like to wait. I'll tell him you'll be out in a few minutes."

Liam had texted. Good thing his mom hadn't noticed. *"[smiling emoji with a halo] Thank you and Happy Thanksgiving."*

Why had Liam chosen the halo emoji to represent Honey? Was it because halo stared with an H or was that the way he saw her? A honey pot would have made more sense, but maybe that was too obvious.

Cici was right, none of the other videos were any better than the one he'd already seen.

"Brayton?" his grandfather said from the doorway.

"Grandpa."

"I thought we were going to have a chat."

"In come."

Grandpa wisely shut the door behind him. "You've seen her recently?"

Brayton nodded. No point in trying to hide it from grandfather with his super nose.

"How recently?"

"Days two. Me rescued."

"Either you haven't taken a shower since then or you did more than just hang around her."

Brayton nodded.

"Brayton! She's a hybrid! Our association with her is already hurting the pack. If you got her pregnant, I'll exile you myself."

Brayton shook his head violently. "No. Happened not that's what." He tapped his chest. "My. Luna."

"WHAT!!!"

"Brayton, I'm here."

*"*Dad ask," he told his grandfather and popped into his wolf form.

His grandfather's mouth, opened for yelling, ended up gaping instead.

Brayton cocked his head at him and sent a message to Honey, *"Hey Honey. Away far how?"*

"Couple of hours."

"Okay you? Saw I fight."

"Yeah. Bullies were trying to make me pay $50 to sleep in my tent for one night. I think they had already terrorized everyone else into paying it."

"Like. Movie."

"They were all human."

He ignored his grandfather's signal for him to change

back.

"*Told. Dad. About. Us.*"

"*You did?*"

"*Dad. Good.*"

"*Wow.*"

"*To Grandpa now speaking.*"

"*I wouldn't think he'd be happy about it.*"

"*No. Care don't.*"

"*Brayton, don't mess up your family relationships because of me.*"

"*You. Family.*"

"*Brayton.*"

"*Let's. Test. Range.*"

"*Far. You talked to me in Australia, remember?*"

"*Did?*"

"*You don't remember?*"

"*Time whole human.*"

"*Well, I heard you. Must have been part of our magic.*"

The words 'our magic' sent a warm, fuzzy feeling rolling through his body. "*Test we.*"

"*I agree,*" she said. "*I'll try talking to you while I'm driving and if I don't hear a response I'll pull over every hundred miles or so and say hi as a wolf.*"

"*Perfect.*"

He could feel Grandpa's alpha power filling the room but he oddly didn't feel the urge to do anything. Some of Honey's resistance must had rubbed off on him too.

"*Must. Go. Careful be.*"

"*I will. Thanks for thinking to put my bike in the shed and for the money and the gear. You did everything perfectly. I especially liked how you put a lock on the inside of the door with a key.*"

He wanted to tell her how much he missed her, but

143

settled with, *"Bye. My. Luna."*

"Goodbye. Happy Thanksgiving."

Too late he remembered he wanted to ask her if she liked gingerbread pumpkin trifle, but that would be too confusing a sentence and she'd probably never heard of it anyway.

Grandpa's face had taken on almost a purple hue. Brayton popped back into his fully clothed human form and rushed to his side. "Okay you?"

"How did you resist me so long and how did you do that so fast and," his grandfather waved his hand up and down, "clothes?"

No way was he going to write out the whole story again. "Ask Dad."

"Does this have something to do with that girl?"

Brayton nodded.

"I'm going to find your dad."

Brayton put two thumbs up.

"Brayton? Oh, good, you found him Alpha Braxton." His mom paused and studied Grandpa's face as he slid past her in the doorway. "Is everything okay?"

"Peachy," Grandpa muttered under his breath.

"Good. Brayton, did you see this video Malcolm found? Doesn't that fighter look a little like Honey?"

Brayton obediently watched the video again, pretending not to notice that his grandfather had stopped with his ear literally in the doorway.

"Guy. Caption. Said."

"Yeah but look, really look, when the fighter turns to yell at everyone. See how they put their head up? That's just like Honey when she's being defiant."

It was. That was probably why he recognized her

144

himself. He made of show of trying to zoom in and get a better look.

"Skinny."

"It's Honey," Mom said with certainty, taking the phone from him. "She probably got caught trying to steal food. She's got to be running low on cash."

"Honey. Not. Thief."

"I'm sure she doesn't want to be, but she's had several near misses lately. She's got to be getting desperate. As soon as she runs out of portals that will be the end and then we can go back to life as normal. In fact, I think the last miss was in Australia. This has to be her! Maybe she's already out of portals." Mom turned to leave the room looking way too excited. "Excuse me Alpha Braxton."

Grandpa peered down the hallway after Brayton's mom for a few seconds, then turned to Brayton, supposedly because Mom was no longer in hearing range. "Was she right?"

"Dad ask."

27

HONEY – NOVEMBER 28 – NORTH AMERICA

Honey followed the camper she'd been drafting behind for the last five miles into the duty-free area. The driver of the camper was a safe driver. The laughing frat guys who'd nearly run her off the road to pass a semi on the right and were now piling boxes of beer into the back of their bright blue Mustang were not. Seriously, how did they think those were all going to fit? Wait a moment, she recognized that logo. They were stocking up on Blue Wolf. Were they wolves or was it the human version of the beer? She loosened the visor to let in more air and possibly their scent. They were wolves. The pack that made Blue Wolf must have decided to expand their label. Good for them. Not so good for American drivers.

She turned into the pump area to top off her tank and scope out her fellow travelers. A semi might work for what she had planned, but they were all on the other side of the lot with their own gas pumps. The camper she'd followed might work too since it had a ladder. She could plant an anchor on the top to pop to later, but they'd parked and the whole family had piled out, including the baby in the stroller. It might be an hour before they came back out. She didn't want to wait that long, plus people might see her climbing up and down the ladder.

A dually truck with Canadian plates pulled into the

spot next to her. The thing was so tall she could barely see into the bed. A big guy in an insulated plaid shirt, a longish beard, and hair curling out from under his baseball cap with a tractor on the front climbed out and gave her a polite nod before moving to the back to fill up his tank. His truck bed would work, if she could find an excuse to touch the inside of the bed.

"How much does that little tank hold, eh?" her neighbor asked.

She pushed up the visor on her helmet to be polite. "3.2 gallons."

He snorted and slapped the edge of his truck bed. "This one holds ten times that but I bet you can go farther on one tank."

She nodded. "I've gotten up to 80 mpg so far, but I was drafting."

"Dangerous."

She shrugged. "You just gotta find a good driver."

"Where you headed? It's Thanksgiving for you folks today, eh?"

"To see some friends." She nonchalantly pulled off her glove and walked into his space and looked into his bed. He had a liner but the paint on the edges of the bed was scratched and worn. She ran her index finger along a scratch and planted an anchor. "Looks like you get a lot of use out of it. I can't haul much with mine."

"Yeah, I should have had the sides lined too."

"Gives it character," she said, turning back to her bike and the pump.

"You gonna be in town long? I hear there's a chance of snow on Sunday."

She looked back over her shoulder, which was hard to

do with the helmet. "I'll keep that in mind. Thanks for the info."

He went back to his business and she attempted to talk to Brayton in human form while waiting for her tank to fill. Again, there was no response. How had he managed before? Was it because he'd been in so much pain? If so, she hoped he never talked to her telepathically while human again.

Not wanting to take off her helmet in front of any cameras or lose sight of her ride into Canada, she drove her bike to the parking lot and pretended to be looking at a phone while she kept an eye on the big truck. The man's tank eventually got full, and after purchasing a very large cup of something, the driver pulled back out onto the road. Honey put away her non-existent phone and pulled out of the parking lot one car behind him.

The long bridge into Canada was just as long as she remembered it, but colder, much colder on her bike. A semi squeezed in between the truck and the car she was following, but she was pretty sure the truck wasn't far ahead.

The closer she got to the border booths, the more her pulse pounded and the more she sweated under her gear despite the cold wind blowing across the bridge. If she couldn't disappear before the border booths came into view, she'd have to show a passport and that would ruin her plans entirely. Would she get a chance to disappear though? With all the construction and the car trying to eat her bumper, there weren't many options.

The truck in front of her had to move right, she took her chance and accelerated so that she was on *his* right, out of sight of the car and hopefully unnoticed by the truck driver.

A moment later she was in the dark of the nether. How long would it take the pick-up to get through the checkpoint? Five minutes? Twenty? She counted to eighteen and nearly pushed off her bike and left it in the nether without anchoring it to herself first. Talk about a disaster. She anchored the palm of her hand to the handlebar, made sure she hadn't forgotten anything else, then sent herself to the bed of the nice Canadian's truck.

The truck was moving past a big semi going the other direction. Neither of them braked. Good, they hadn't seen her. Even better, the truck wasn't moving very fast which meant he hadn't hit the main road yet. Now if he'd just stop at a light.

The bottom of a bridge went by overhead and the truck sped up. Had she waited too long in the nether? Had he already passed all the stop lights she remembered from when her grandmother had drove along the same road last spring? At least the sun was in the right spot, meaning they were going the right direction. As if he'd heard her, the driver slowed and looped around what felt like a full circle. Now the winter sun was mostly on her left. He turned again, truly north this time, then slowed and did a U-turn. A store with a huge 'Costco' sign came into view over the edge of the bed. Perfect. As soon as the truck stopped, she sent herself to the nether for five more seconds which should be at least 3 minutes on Earth, then sent herself back. A few seconds later and she was beside the truck and on her bike like she'd been there the whole time.

"Honey?"

Shoot. She'd forgotten about Brayton. He was probably wondering what was taking so long. She drove out of the lot and turned into an abandoned parking lot, then rolled to a stop behind a small brick building. Making sure no one was looking, she sent the bike back to the nether and transformed at the same time.

"Here."

The Costco must be on the very edge of town. To her east was nothing but wide-open fields.

"Grandpa hear?"

"What?"

"Can. You. Hear. Grandpa?"

"No. He knows?"

"Yes."

"And?"

"Mad not."

"That's good. Why did you tell him?" His grandpa hated her.

"Smelled. You. On. Me."

"And you couldn't think of some excuse?"

"No. Wants. Plan."

"Why?"

"My. Luna. Family."

"And you trust him?"

"Yes."

"He wants to help even though he was right about me being a witch?"

"To family loyal."

Right, because that worked out so well with Brayton's mom. *"Tell him I'm trying to break the curse and if he has any way to go deep sea diving and collect something off the ocean floor, that would be very helpful."* That should keep him busy.

"Okay."

"He said that?"

"No. Write. Long."

"You have to write everything out and it will take a long time?"

"Yes."

"I better get back on the road. I want to be there before things close."

"Texas. Far."

"I'm not going to Texas. I had a change of plans. Hopefully this will work better."

"Safe?"

"Yes. Safer than Texas."

"Eat."

"I will."

"Now."

She rolled her eyes, but she *was* getting hungry. "I'll find a drive-through, bossy, and I'll talk to you again in another hour or so."

"Careful."

"I'll be careful." She swore she could feel his concern. Did telepathy work that way?

After she'd transformed and downed some food, she got back on the main road and followed the signs to the highway. The blue Mustang passed her a few miles later with the trunk tied down with a long-sleeve shirt. About twenty miles later, she passed the same car parked on the side between two cop cars with their lights flashing. Two of the four boys were kneeling on the ground with their hands zip-tied behind their backs. The other two were being processed. They weren't laughing any more. In fact, they looked awfully grim for a speeding ticket.

Served them right for driving so recklessly.

Why were they zip-tied though? They hadn't been driving *that* fast and beer was legal, or else they wouldn't sell it at the border.

And why had the policemen looked so happy? Were they excited about Blue Wolf?

Something wasn't right.

Shaking her head at her nosiness, she took the next exit. As soon as she was sure there were no other vehicles around to see her, she drove behind some bushes and changed into her wolf form.

The cops and the boys were still there by the time she'd run back the mile or so through the fields. She hid her smell with a shield and crept through the tall grass to listen. One of the cops turned her way and looked in her direction. Had he heard her, or had he felt her? She couldn't exactly wear her I'm-a-witch charm when she was in wolf form, not unless she pulled her sports top out of the nether. He took a couple of steps her way. She popped her bra on. As long as nobody saw her, it wouldn't matter. The cop took a few more steps, then paused.

"Blake, what are you looking at?" the cop looming over the now-empty trunk of the mustang called. All the beer was stacked to the side of the car.

"Nothing."

"Then come help me. I found something in the tire well."

"You did not. There's nothing in there but the tire," one of the boys yelled.

The second cop leaned into the trunk. The wind wasn't blowing the right way for Honey to smell magic, but she was high enough on the bank that she could see the black of the tire disappear and become white.

"Well, well, well," the first cop said, holding up a quart-sized bag of white powder, "Nothing indeed."

"You planted that!" the boy yelled.

"Prove it. The camera doesn't lie."

"There's more," the second cop said, holding up several bags in each hand. "More than enough for a drug trafficking charge. You boys are going away for a long time."

"What do you want," one of the other boys demanded.

"We already got it. Call it in."

"This won't stick. Everyone will be able to tell you're lying," another boy said.

"Not if you confess, and you will confess, because you did it," the first cop said, a nasty grin on his face as he approached them. "I better check those ties."

Honey switched to her other sight. The cop raised his hand over the first boy's head. She didn't know what his magic-packed class ring was about to do, but since he wasn't supposed to be doing magic on wolves, Honey felt justified in slicing through the spell with a modified shield.

The second cop immediately looked her way. She tried to freeze the cops, but neither one appeared affected. In another moment, she had their shield charms disabled and tried again. The second cop halted in mid step like a plastic soldier. Funny. She froze the frat boys next. Yeah, she was using magic on them, but she wasn't trying to harm them.

Now what should she do? From the few cop shows she'd seen, she knew if there was no evidence the boys couldn't be charged. That meant getting rid of the drugs, the cameras, and their recordings. Hmmm.

She looked up and down the highway, and, seeing no one, quickly ran down the bank and brushed against the cop car facing the open trunk to send it to the nether. That should at least make the recording screwed up and prevent anyone from seeing her. With her magic sight, she scanned the scene. There was nothing magical about the bag of drugs cop 1 was holding up, so it wasn't an illusion. That meant the second cop must have either transmuted the spare tire into drugs or they had a stock of drugs in the nether. She didn't see any tethers on the bag the first cop was holding, but maybe the second cop had already removed them. She tapped the bag of drugs, reluctantly putting her own tether on it just before she sent it to the nether. She did the same for the bags the second cop was holding, then made sure the tire well and the truck were empty. She'd figure out how to destroy the bags later.

Now cameras. She went back to where she'd been when she'd brushed against the car and pulled it back from the nether. From outside the passenger window, she could see a little black box near the rear-view mirror that might be a camera, but there was a lot of other equipment to contend with. Who knew cop cars came with laptops? Did that mean the video had already been sent somewhere? If so, destroying the camera and the recording wouldn't help at all. She sent the car back to the nether again.

What should she do? If the video evidence still existed, destroying the drugs wouldn't help because the cops would just make more drugs to replace what she'd taken. The only way to stop that was to bind the cop's powers, but then they'd know someone had been there.

What if the boys ran? No. That wouldn't solve anything, it would make it worse.

Binding the cops was the only way. Not forever

though. It didn't feel right to make it permanent.

After freezing all of them again, she walked up to one of the cops and touched him with her nose. Imagining the spell wrapping around him like twine, she thought, *"Because you attempted to plant false evidence against wolves, I bind your powers until you voluntarily, out of the goodness of your heart, help a wolf."* In her imagination, she pulled the knot nice and tight behind his neck.

She did the same thing to the other cop, except she took away his ability to cast spells or use spells and charms made by others.

Was it too harsh? She felt suddenly weaker and stumbled back. Sending a car to the nether a couple of times must take a lot of power. Now she needed a nap.

First though, she had to get rid of the drugs.

Did she though? If the boys' minds couldn't be altered and cop 2 couldn't make more drugs…she grinned to herself. One by one, she put the bags back, complete with a large hole in each corner. The breeze was blowing away from her and the wolves and towards the cops until a semi went by, then it blew everywhere, including on her. Yuck.

Holding her breath, she put the car back, then sent herself back to the bush she'd picked as a tether. The grass behind the bush looked extremely comfortable. Maybe she should take a nap. No, she scolded herself. They might be able to track her from the scene since she ran there. One more hour, she promised herself after she transformed back into a human sitting on a bike, then she could rest.

28

HONEY – NOVEMBER 28 – CANADA

The mall closed at 6 pm. It didn't matter that Honey made it with ten minutes to spare despite her hour-long nap, because the girl who made the magic slates was gone, completely. Her tiny little store was now manned by a boy selling pet rocks with emoji faces that changed depending on how well you were caring for them. Cute but not something she needed. They would make good Christmas gifts though. Luca would probably like it, Frederica too. She needed to save her money but…she bought two.

Back outside the mall, she looked up and down the sidewalk debating what to do. The magic slates were the whole reason she'd driven to Canada. They were key to her plan to contact Vera Lambert, the young water witch in Texas, without alerting or getting captured by the complex hologram aunt spell that watched over Vera's witch college.

The slate girl's grandmother/librarian would likely know where she'd gone, but there was a danger the nice older librarian would recognize Honey even if she wore a disguise since she'd spent so much time in the library last summer. She did still have that disguise charm she was supposed to use in Boston. No, she wouldn't use that yet. Frederica should be in school now and that was only a few blocks away. Slate girl was Frederica's cousin and it would be nice to see Frederica again.

She dug into her backpack to find a pen and a notebook then wrote two messages, one for if Frederica was at the school and one for if she wasn't. A few minutes later, her bike was parked by the curb and finger was on the school's doorbell. She was positive no one would recognize her in her motorcycle gear.

"Yes?"

Shoot. Of all the people to answer the door it had to be Miss Evelstone. Honey wished she'd thought to bring a clipboard or a sheet of paper so she'd have an excuse to look down. She blinked her brown contacts into place behind her barely tinted helmet shield, cleared her throat, and spoke deeply.

"Good afternoon. I have a delivery for a Miss Frederica Felix."

"I can sign."

"I am to deliver it directly to her."

"And who shall I say you are with?"

"The Caring Courier Company," Honey made-up on the spot.

"Wait here please."

What would a professional courier do? Honey decided to turn her back on the door, which probably had a camera or the magical equivalent of one aimed right at her and pretended to be interested in the street.

After several minutes, the door finally opened. "She doesn't appear to be in," Miss Evelstone said, "but her sister is here."

"I must deliver the package only to the requested recipient. Would you please make sure she gets this," Honey handed over the paper that said she'd try again at 8 am in the morning. "Thank you."

"What is it?" Frederica's sister asked. "Who sent it?"

Honey pretended not to hear and walked purposely to her bike. Riding away like she had a place to go, she considered what to do next. Going to the school had been an absolute failure plus she had almost exposed herself. Knowing Frederica, she had portalled to visit the guys for Thanksgiving, all without Ms. Charming's knowledge of course. Honey hoped she hadn't gotten Frederica in trouble. On the plus side, if she *was* with the boys, then Honey could write to them and maybe communicate with Frederica that way, assuming the guys checked the slate while they were busy stuffing themselves with turkey.

Food first though. Whether it was riding her bike or the cold or the last few months catching up to her, she didn't know, but she hadn't felt so empty in a long while. Spaghetti and meatballs sounded heavenly, and she knew just the place to go.

"Isabelle, is that you?"

Honey peered up from the huge meatball she was stuffing into her mouth at the muscular dark-skinned girl standing over her. "Rrrmrrr?"

Rosemary, her friend and former co-worker laughed and slid into the other side of the booth. "It is you. Oh my gosh. I thought you'd died or something."

"Nnn," Honey said through the napkin while she tried to chew and wipe her face at the same time.

Ethan, another co-worker squeezed in next to Rosemary, not that he had much choice since she was holding his hand.

"Are you two dating now?" Honey asked after finally swallowing.

Rosemary held up their linked hands and grinned. "He finally wore me down."

"How many cups of coffee did it take?"

"About a swimming pool full, but it was worth it," Ethan smiled.

Rosemary rolled her eyes, but her face was all smiles too, until it wasn't. She crossed her arms and gave Honey a stern look.

"Okay, tell me. What happened to you?"

"What did the headmistress of the school say?"

"She said it was a family emergency and that it was highly unlikely you would be back."

Good excuse. She could work with that.

"She was right. I didn't expect to come back at all."

"How long have you been in town?"

Honey looked at her watch. "About one hour."

"How long are you staying?"

"I don't know. Not long. I'm just here to speak with someone."

"Are the meatballs good today?"

"Delicious."

"Ethan?"

Her blond boyfriend kissed her cheek. "On it babe." Rosemary waited for him to reach the counter before turning back to Honey.

"Are you okay?"

"Yeah."

"You lost weight."

"Why does everyone keep saying that?"

"Because you did. Like a lot of weight."

"Not on purpose. I was doing a lot of running."

"Training for a marathon?"

"Something like that."

"Where are you going to school now?"

"I'm not." Honey stabbed at another meatball. She wanted to go to school, desperately. It made her mad and sad whenever she thought about it, which was why she tried not to.

"You dropped out?"

"Not by choice."

"Do you want to talk about it?"

Honey gave her friend a grateful smile. "There's not really much to talk about, but thanks for asking. Hopefully everything works out and I can go back to school soon."

Rosemary traced a scratch in the table, then said, "There's a missing child poster of a girl named Honey that looks just like you hanging in the grocery."

Honey started rolling pasta around her fork as nonchalantly as she could. "Really? I must have doppelganger. I'll have to go by and look."

"She's a year younger than you, but she's also from Indiana."

"Odd," she said through the pasta now in her mouth. "Maybe she's a long-lost cousin or something. I don't know much about my mom's side of the family."

Rosemary tilted her head and gave Honey a patient look. "Isabelle, tell me the truth."

"I haven't lied to you."

"You have to know I won't report you, not unless I thought you were in danger or something."

Continue to deny or let Rosemary in? She hated this, this keeping secrets from friends and family. How had her parents kept it up for so long?

"I trust you Rosemary, but there are a lot of things

160

going on that I can't explain – that I'm not allowed to explain. What I can tell you is that the people looking for me mean me harm. Those posters weren't put up by my parents. My family knows where I am and what I'm doing."

"What are you, from a family of spies or something?"

"Something."

"Mafia?"

"That's closer."

"Italian mafia?"

"No, more like old-fashioned secret societies with oddball beliefs."

"Like the thing with the triangle and the eye."

"You mean the Eye of Providence?"

"Sure," Rosemary agreed, nodding and shaking her head at once so that it moved mostly in a circle.

"The Illuminati symbol," Honey threw out.

"Yes! That's it!"

"Are we sharing conspiracy theories," Ethan asked, sliding into the booth beside Rosemary.

"No, it's a trivia question," Rosemary said, turning to him. "What is the name of the eye in the triangle?"

"You mean the Eye of Providence?"

Rosemary huffed and turned her back to him.

"What? That's right isn't it?"

"Yes," Honey said, grinning at Rosemary's antics.

"If that was a sports question, I would have nailed it. I know," Rosemary said, visibly brightening, "We could have trivia night. Want to come over and play?"

"I'd love to," Honey said honestly. "Don't you have class tomorrow though?"

Rosemary shrugged. "My first class isn't until ten."

161

"Am I invited too?" Ethan asked.

"Of course. You can be on my brother's team."

Ethan made a face. "He doesn't even answer the sports questions right."

"He's bound to answer something right eventually."

"Honey?"

She appreciated being able to talk to Brayton with just a thought, she really did, but did he have to call so often and right when she had a nearly full plate of spaghetti in front of her?

"I'm eating you dimwit. Stop calling me!"

"Me just dimwit call did you a?"

"You heard that?"

"Yeah."

He didn't sound hurt, but she knew somehow that he was.

"I'm sorry. I didn't mean it. I didn't think you could hear me. I was about to devour a big plate of spaghetti and I didn't want to leave it to transform in the bathroom."

"Now human?"

"Yeah."

"Are talking how me to you?"

"I don't know. I did try talking to you as a human while I was riding today, but maybe you have to be a wolf to hear."

"Becoming again never human I'm."

"Brayton, don't be ridiculous," she rolled her eyes.

"Isabelle, what are you doing?" Rosemary asked.

Honey hid her half-full mouth with her hand before she asked, "What do you mean?"

"I don't think I've ever seen anyone eat that fast."

"This is really good."

"Thanksgiving. Food. Good. Trifle made gingerbread

162

grandmother pumpkin."

"And you were mumbling to yourself."

"A what?" she sent to Brayton before mumbling to Rosemary, "The Yoda in my head chose now to have a conversation."

"Dessert favorite."

"OSV," Ethan supplied.

"What's that mean?" Rosemary asked.

"Object-subject-verb. That's how Yoda speaks."

"I call Ethan for my team," Honey declared before Rosemary could.

"Team? Who Ethan?" Brayton asked.

"Friends. Human. Trivial Pursuit," she sent rapidly. *"I'll have to talk to you later so they don't think I'm crazy. I'm in a restaurant."*

"Eating?"

"Yes."

"Lot?"

"Yes."

"Good. Wolf sleep as. Fun have you."

29

HONEY - NOVEMBER 29 - CANADA

"I really appreciate you doing this," Honey said when Rosemary let her out of the car a couple of blocks from the witch school.

"No problem. I feel like a spy or something."

"Remember, you are from the Caring Courier Company and don't forget to check her ID before you make your delivery."

"I've got it. Man, it's cold. I can't believe you rode a motorbike up here yesterday and were planning to camp. Shut the door already."

"Yes, Mom."

Honey headed across the street toward an insurance agency after Rosemary drove away. Once she hit the sidewalk, she turned toward the park two blocks down. The coat Rosemary's brother had grown out of was roomy on her and with a hood over her beanie and the collar up, the only skin exposed to the cold was around her eyes. She was pretty sure no one would recognize her even if they were looking right at her.

Had Frederica signed for her Thanksgiving card yet and read the message on the signature sheet? How long would it take for her to get to the human library?

Honey had just reached the corner of the park when she heard the engine of Rosemary's old clunker approaching from behind. Rosemary stopped at the light and Honey slipped smoothly into the car.

"How did it go? Did she say what time she'll meet me?"

Rosemary frowned up at the stoplight. "She wasn't there."

"Did they say where she was?"

"No, but they seemed surprised she was missing."

"Did you say when you'd be back?"

"No, I told them I would confer with the sender."

"Good idea."

Honey slumped back into the seat. Where could Frederica be? Had her sister made her disappear again or had someone else decided to start torturing her friends? She quickly scanned Rosemary for any signs of tracking spells or other magic. Nothing.

"What do you want to do now?" Rosemary asked.

"Just drop me off like we planned. I need to contact some people and see if I can figure out if she's in trouble or just took an impromptu vacation."

"You think she'd do that – take a vacation I mean?"

"I don't know," Honey said honestly. "Thanks for your help though and for letting me stay over last night. It was much better than camping."

"Of course it was. You're welcome to stay with me as long as you are in town."

"I really appreciate that. I don't know what my plans are yet though."

"Well, you know where to find me. I've got work tonight."

"Thanks Rosemary, and if anyone questions you about me, just tell the truth, although if you can think of a way not to tell them about my bike, I would appreciate it."

"Sure."

Rosemary turned into a parking lot. As soon as she was sure anyone following them couldn't see her next move, Honey jumped out and put distance between herself and the car.

"Brayton?"

No answer. He must not be in wolf form. She would have to transform, but where?. She darted across the four-lane street on the opposite side of the parking lot towards a strip of restaurants. Unfortunately, none were opened yet except…she turned right and walked for another block. Her nose was correct, there was a Starbucks. She made a beeline for the bathroom, then stood on the toilet seat and transformed in one of the empty stalls.

"Brayton, Frederica isn't at school. Can you check with the guys and see if they've seen her? If not, tell Luca to contact her dad and ask him. I'm worried about her. Let me know please."

The bathroom door opened. Honey quickly transformed again and exited the stall past a little girl and her mom.

"Mom, why is there a boy in the girl's bathroom?"

"Maybe he got confused."

Ha. She'd fooled two people at least. Next time she should use the men's room.

Where to, she wondered when she stepped back out on the sidewalk. Was it safe to go to the witch library and ask the grandmother/librarian about her granddaughter's business? The woman had been really kind, and it would be nice to get out of the cold and read while she waited for Brayton's response. A thought struck her so hard she had to stop in the middle of the sidewalk for a moment. She could look up water retrieval spells!

166

30

BRAYTON – NOVEMBER 29 – INDIANA

Brayton had just stuck a forkful of eggs in his mouth when Honey's voice sounded in his head. *"Brayton, Frederica isn't at school. Can you check with the guys and see if they've seen her? If not, tell Luca to contact her dad and ask him. I'm worried about her. Let me know please."*

"Do they taste okay Brayton?"

Mom was literally hovering over him. Ever since he'd run back from hiding Honey's bike, his mom had stuck to him like his own personal rain cloud. It was driving him nuts.

"Mom. Here. Why?" She always shopped on Black Friday, always.

Mom sat down in the chair beside him with a sigh. "You mean why am I not shopping?"

He nodded.

"I wasn't in the mood. Besides, you're meeting with Mrs. Wixx today, right? I'm going with you."

"No."

"Yes. I am not going to let another witch kidnap you or get her hands on you."

"Witch Wixx," he reminded her.

"Well, except for her. She's the one witch I trust not

167

to torture you for information on that girl since she probably knows exactly where she is. Maybe I should torture her."

"Mom!"

Mom patted Brayton's arm. "Just kidding. Really though, I don't know why they're going after you when she's more likely to know something."

"Doesn't. Sad," Brayton couldn't help saying. As far as he knew Mrs. Wixx had only spoken to Honey when she drove her to Canada. With all the witches she lived with, it wasn't safe to even have a magic slate.

"I guess I would be too if I had a grandchild I didn't know existed until a year ago and I couldn't even enjoy them because they were, well what that girl is." She pointed a finger at his nose. "Don't you do that to me, Brayton."

He would have pointed out how extremely unlikely that was given how she was hovering, but it was more trouble than it was worth to try and put the sentence together.

"Where are you meeting her, at the library again?"

Brayton nodded.

"It would be better if she meets you here. I'll send someone to pick her up."

"No."

"Yes!"

"No." He tapped his head. "Favor. Two. More. Hours. Road on. Much too ask to." Plus, he wouldn't be able to pass a message onto Honey's friends, assuming they could visit the campus today.

"It was one of her own who did this to you, I don't think it's too much to ask."

"Her not. Ours Damien."

"Don't even. Damien is a whole other story." She picked up her phone. "I'll send Bernadette to get her."

"No!" Brayton said more firmly.

His mom's finger shook where it hovered above the screen, but it didn't get any closer. She looked up at him with her eyes wide with shock.

"Did you just use alpha power on me?"

Oops. "Maybe."

"Brayton Maxwell Mooney, you know better than that. You don't use alpha power on your mother, ever. That's it. You're grounded."

He pointed at himself. "Nineteen. Adult. College."

"As long as you live in *my* house you will abide by *my* rules."

He shoveled the last of his eggs into his mouth, wiped his face with a napkin, and took his plate to the sink.

Mom had her phone out again. For a moment he debated using the full-strength of his newfound power to not only get her off his back but to get her to stop pursuing Honey. Then he thought of how his father would react. Alphas didn't like it when other alphas messed with their Lunas. He understood that even better now.

He took the phone away from his mom as gently as his growing irritation with her would allow, then put it face down on the table in front of her.

"No," he said again, but kept his powers in check. "I. Go. Alone."

"You're grounded."

"Leaving."

"What?"

"Packing," he said to make his intentions explicitly

clear. "House your. Mine not. Goodbye."

"No Brayton, it's not safe. Where will you go?"

He gave her a sly smile like he had a plan, then left her fuming in her chair. Unfortunately, she didn't fume long. She followed him around his room alternately berating him and attempting to coax him not to leave for the next ten minutes while he threw everything he thought would be useful into his backpack. He already had his backpack slung over his shoulder when he remembered the sleeping bag and pup tent his mom had bought him when he was twelve in the top of the closet. He pulled those down, stuffed them into his pillowcase along with his pillow, and scooped his keys off his desk.

He mom planted herself in his doorway and crossed her arms. "You are not leaving."

"Move."

"Not until we talk about this."

"Talk can't," he tapped his head. "Appointment."

"Don't give me that. It's not for another couple of hours."

"Go I. Here stay you."

"Brayton you're being childish. I've taken you to nearly every doctor's visit you've gone to. This is no different."

"Move."

"I'm your mother, Brayton. I know what's best for you."

Her smug look only made the building alpha power harder to control. If she didn't move soon, he was going to overpower her and possibly do something irrevocable to her memory.

"Brayton?"

170

Honey's voice was like a balm to the turmoil brewing inside of him.

He closed his eyes and willed his thoughts to hers as hard as he could. *"Of here me get out."*

"I'm coming."

"No! Me pull."

"I don't know if that will work, but I will try. Hold your breath."

31

"What happened?" Honey asked, stepping back to take a look at Brayton. He appeared unharmed. "Why are you holding your pillow and your backpack?"

"Mom."

"You'll have to give me more than that."

"Stubborn. Leave I to wanted. Let she not."

"You wanted to leave and she wouldn't let you?"

He nodded.

"And you got into a fight?"

He nodded again.

"And you had me pull you out of there instead of finding a way to work out your differences."

He nodded.

She put her hands on her hips and stared him down. "Brayton."

"Tried." He grabbed her upper arm and tugged her toward him. "Made mad me. Her afraid hurt I'd."

"Like you did me?" she asked softly.

He nodded, his eyes pleading for understanding while his hands slid down her arms to grab her hands. His forehead contacted hers next and he took a deep breath.

"You okay?"

He nodded against her head. "You missed I."

"I know."

His lips found hers and she remembered why she liked

172

kissing him so much. At least a minute passed before he pulled away with a shiver to study their surroundings.

"Where?"

"Abandoned farmhouse near London, Canada. I thought this would be better than the library I was in. Do you have a coat?"

He shook his head and lifted up his pillowcase. "Sleeping bag."

"You'll need more than that." She started to take off the coat that had been gifted to her, but Brayton stopped her and popped into his wolf form.

Honey sat on the dusty floor beside him and put her arm over his shoulders. "You're still going to be cold if your winter fur hasn't come in. Did you get a chance to ask Luca about Frederica?"

"No. Plan. See. Your Grandmother. Speak. Then."

"On campus?"

He nodded. *"Need. Ask. First."*

She leaned her head up against his. "Wonder what your mom is doing now that you disappeared."

"Care don't."

"Yes you do." She kissed his furry cheek, "but I understand. My mom and I didn't always agree on everything."

"Didn't?"

"Nope. I would argue. She would listen, then we'd do what she wanted." Honey sighed. "I would give anything to see her again, even if it was just to argue."

He nuzzled her cheek and she didn't try to stop the tears that fell. He'd seen her cry before. This was nothing.

He whined. She wiped her tears away and smiled at him. "Don't worry, I'm not going to drown you. Was my

173

grandmother going to try and heal you?"

"*Yes.*"

"We better get you there then. Where shall I take you: shed or guys?"

"*Shed. Run will home I. Time have.*"

"You sure?"

"*Yes. Littles visit grandma after.*"

"Do you have time to do it before? I'm worried about Frederica."

"*Maybe.*"

She hugged him. "You ready?"

"*Wait.*"

She abruptly had her arm around a human Brayton who plopped his now human behind onto the floor and pulled her into his lap to give her a very thorough kiss.

32

BRAYTON – 9 AM – INDIANA

"Brayton, where are you son?" Grandpa's voice sounded in his head just as he jumped a fallen tree. Mom had gotten his grandparents involved? Seeing him disappear must have really scared her.

"Coming."

"You're okay?"

"Yes."

"Who took you?"

"No one. Left I. Mom stubborn."

"This has been really hard on your mom."

"Understand."

"She just wants to protect you."

"Know I."

"She said you were moving out."

"Yes."

"She said you used alpha power on her."

"Yes. Why leaving."

"Are you having trouble controlling your new power?"

"Only. Around. Mom."

"Ah."

Several pack members in wolf form ran out of the trees to join him.

"How about I go with you to your appointment. I'd like to meet this Mrs. Wixx."

"Too come Grandmother."

"Afraid I will scare the witch?"

"Yes."

His grandpa laughed. *"If she is anything like Honey, I doubt it."*

"Okay. Honey. My. Luna?"

"If she can break the curse, I have no issue with it. She's a brave, intelligent, if stubborn girl. She'll make a good Luna."

"Thanks Grandpa."

Brayton led the wolves who'd joined him along the trail by the creek where the trees and tall grass provided cover in case any humans were watching, then through the gate into the fenced-in yard where no delivery people or unexpected visitors could see. His mom, who was waiting for him in human form, ran to hug him the moment he emerged.

"Brayton, where were you? I was so worried." She sniffed, then pulled back so she could look him in the eye. "And why do you smell like that girl? Is she responsible for this?"

The way she said it, with such disgust and anger, as if Honey could help being what she was, pissed him off worse than he'd been before. Without thinking how his pack might react to his new ability, he transformed in front of her and the pack members in the yard complete with his backpack and pillowcase.

"Disappearing for me? No." Dang it all, he'd forgotten he couldn't talk properly. He could still get his point across though. "Honey. My. Luna. Leave. Her. Alone!"

His mom's slap didn't hurt so much as seal his decision to move out. She covered her mouth and started to apologize, but he'd had enough. He stepped back away from her, then walked around her into the house past all the wolves in both furry and human form to stop in front of his grandfather's wolf waiting just by the door.

"Coming?"

"Wouldn't miss it."

"Tell me what happened today," Grandpa said ten minutes later from the passenger seat.

"When?"

"When you disappeared."

"Nothing."

"Brayton, my nose tells me something happened."

Was that because he could smell Honey or him or because he was smelling the lie?

"Kissed," he admitted.

"No kidding. What I meant was, how did you disappear? Is that part of your new magic?"

"Maybe?"

"You don't know?"

"No."

"Where did you go?"

"Canada."

"Is that where Honey is now?"

"Know I don't," he said honestly. She probably had popped back to the library, because, well, it was a library and she was Honey.

"Can she make portals?" Grandmother asked from the back seat.

"No."

"Then how did you go to Canada and back so fast?"

"Know don't I."

"I really hope this Mrs. Wixx can help you, Yoda."

"Grandpa!"

"Braxton, don't pick on the boy," Grandmother

177

scolded. "He's a mated man now."

Brayton felt the red creeping up his neck. "Haven't we... We. Haven't."

"I'm not talking about sex Brayton. She picked you and you've clearly picked her or else you wouldn't share her powers."

"Young."

"Doesn't matter."

Brayton's phone started playing the theme song he'd chosen for Honey's friends.

"Who is that? That sounds like the three stooges," Grandpa said.

Brayton pushed a button on his SUV console. "Hello?"

"*Brayton, turn on WTV,*" Luca's frantic voice came through the speaker.

"Driving."

"What's wrong?" Grandpa asked.

"*Alpha Braxton?*"

"Yes."

"*The witch down in Texas has Frederica. She trapped her in a cursed crystal. She's sending out a challenge to Honey to come and prove once and for all that she is a curse breaker. She said Frederica will die inside the crystal without food or water.*"

"Write?" Brayton asked.

"*Yeah, but you know she's slow to respond. Do you have a faster way?*"

"Yeah." Brayton flipped on his signal and pulled over as far as he could to the side of the road. "Grandpa. Drive. Grandma. Front."

He waited until they were on the road again with him in the backseat before he transformed and sent, "*Honey.*

Me come to."

A few seconds later she was in the seat next to him with her lips on his human ones, but only for a moment.

"What's wrong?"

"*Those crazy witches in Texas cursed Frederica!*" Luca yelled through the phone.

"*Give me the phone,*" Nathan said in the background.

"*She's got to save her,*" Luca insisted.

"*She has to know what happened first,*" Nathan said, his voice getting louder, likely because he was taking control of the phone. "*According to the news, Frederica went down to Texas to try and talk the Texas witches into giving up their part of the curse. They trapped her in a cursed crystal instead without food or water and put out a challenge to you. They said if you prove you're a curse breaker by freeing her, they'll give you their part of the curse.*"

"Trap," Brayton said.

"Most likely," Honey agreed, "but I have to free her. There's no one else."

"I bet there's a way to do it without breaking the curse," his grandmother said.

"Probably," Honey agreed, "but if they want proof, I'll give them proof."

"*Maybe she'll just portal out.*" Nathan said.

"I'm sure that's the first thing she tried. Do you guys have her dad's phone number?"

"Does Dad," Brayton said.

"Good. Tell your dad to contact Frederica's dad and tell him to come here. Actually, tell him to go wherever you're going." Honey leaned closer to the phone. "You guys watch the news and try and figure out where the crystal is currently placed and how they're likely to ambush me. I'll research the crystal. Call Brayton in one hour.

179

Don't worry, I'll get her out. Hang up now."

Grandpa pushed the button to hang up the phone, then asked, "What's your plan?"

"Snatch the crystal and break her out on camera in another place so they can't trap me. Do you know some wolves with cameras you can trust, maybe someone who works at a station so there is no question that I really did break her out?"

"I do."

"Good, tell them to get their gear together. As soon as Mr. Felix is here, he can portal them to a safe spot where the witches won't be."

"How about a TV station?" Grandpa suggested.

"That will work." Honey leaned forward and picked up a penny and a nickel from the center console, then casually pressed the nickel to her left cheek and the penny to her right. "You and Mr. Felix should visit the station first so he knows where to portal to after I grab the crystal." She handed Brayton the nickel, "then have him portal you and Brayton to Texas and as close as you can to where they have the crystal." She handed Brayton the penny, then leaned closer like she was going to kiss his cheek and whispered, "Face up, just in case."

"Where will you be?" Grandpa asked.

"I'll be waiting for Brayton to describe the situation in Texas." She slipped some hairbands off her wrists and handed them to Brayton. "Shield charms for all of you and one for Mr. Felix."

"You seem very confident," Grandma said.

"Because anything else won't work."

Brayton couldn't stand to be so close and not touch her anymore. He put his arm around her and pulled her against his shoulder in a one-armed hug.

"Honey, take off your hat," Grandfather requested firmly, his eyes on the rear-view mirror instead of the road.

She reached up and plucked it off her head as requested. "I cut my hair. It's easier to care for this way."

"Oh!" Grandma said, covering her mouth with both hands. "Her marks do glow."

Brayton elbowed her. "Show. Wolf."

Honey rolled her eyes at him, then abruptly, a beautiful, white, faintly glowing animal with the same green eyes was beside him.

"Oh my," Grandma said.

"She was a different color before, wasn't she?" Grandpa asked.

"Yes," Brayton said.

"Does she always glow?" Grandma asked.

Honey turned human again and answered, "So far. It makes it difficult to hide at night, though."

"You poor dear. Oh look, Brayton's marks are glowing now too. What does it mean, Braxton?"

"It means every Tom, Dick, and wanna-be alpha is going to be after Brayton's mate," his grandpa growled. "You just had to pick a special one, didn't you boy?"

"She. Pick. Me!"

Grandpa snorted. "Right, Mr. Mooney, and I mean that just like it sounds. Little Luna, you best go do your research, I think we've got company coming," he nodded at the lights flashing in the side mirror. "Probably heard your voice on the phone."

"Probably," she agreed, then touched her hand to Brayton's cheek. "Stay safe. Call me if you need me."

181

He leaned closer to kiss her goodbye, but she was already gone.

33

HONEY - AFTER 9 AM - CANADA

Honey rode her bike as close as she could get to the magical library on campus, then rolled it between a bush and a building and sent it and her helmet into the nether. While behind the bush she donned her blond wig, beanie, silk scarf, big frames, and long, flowy skirt. Paired with Rosemary's brother's jacket it made for an eclectic costume. Now if she could pull off a British accent, it might be enough to keep the librarian from recognizing her.

The wall where several ancient computers were housed around the entrance to the magical library was way more crowded than usual. At least seven students were shoulder-to-shoulder around one monitor talking with hushed voices, but not hushed enough to prevent Honey from hearing them when she passed by.

"He's not moving."

"Do you think he's dead?"

"Is it really him? Maybe it's her in disguise."

"What's happened?" Honey asked one of the students on the fringe.

He frowned at her. Guessing he was suspicious because she was a stranger, she made the molecules around his face shift so he'd know she was a witch. Still frowning, he shifted over just enough that she could see half the screen.

The room on the screen looked familiar, but it took her a moment to identify it as the library at the school in Texas. All the furniture had been pushed to the edges except for a small table on which sat a large green crystal held up point first in a claw-like metal holder. A balding man lay unmoving on the floor next to the table, reaching toward the table.

"That's Mr. Felix. What happened to him?"

"You know him?" the young man next to her asked.

"Yeah. He let me test one of his port-a-corns. He's really nice."

"Not too smart though. He portalled to his daughter and sprung the trap set for the hybrid. Stupid. Now she'll know what to expect."

What was wrong with this person? "Of course he did. It's his daughter. Besides, what makes you think the hybrid even knows what's going on? She's in hiding. She probably doesn't have access to the news."

He held up his cell phone, "They sent out an emergency alert. Unless she's living under a rock, she knows."

"You have clearly never watched a single detective show. If she's smart, which she has to be to have stayed free so long, she ditched her cell phone first thing so no one could track her."

"You know those shows are all fiction, right."

"Based on fact."

She pushed a little closer to the screen and focused with her magic sight. To her surprise, she could see lines of magic flowing around Mr. Felix and forming a cocoon. Which, she realized after a moment, did make sense, because there was way too much magic in that building for

184

normal cameras to work. The magical creation that was Philomena Lambert must be responsible for the footage. Oddly, the crystal barely glowed at all.

"Have they given any history on the crystal?" she asked the girl sitting in front of the monitor.

"No. They think Madame Lambert cursed it just to catch the hybrid."

"Which Madame Lambert?"

"The one that wears really old clothes, Philomena I think," the girl said, distractedly typing something in another window.

Could a spell make a curse? Philomena was a very complicated spell herself and had access to all kinds of magic, but Honey doubted she *made* any of it. The young Ms. Lambert or her mother could have cursed the crystal, but a good curse required either a lot of hate or a lot of conviction. The young Ms. Lambert had been nice and eager to make a new friend. It was hard to envision her hating someone enough to make a strong curse, especially to trap someone as friendly as Frederica.

What if Frederica wasn't in the crystal? She might not even be in the room. Was she even cursed?

It didn't matter. She was going to have to go there to rescue Mr. Felix now. Honey scanned all the books and the objects lining the library shelves for suspicious magic while the students muttered and moved around her. The view changed before she was done to show a different angle which included the fireplace complete with a cheery little magical fire. Above the mantel was a picture of two girls having a tea party. She didn't remember that from her visit and certainly didn't remember the bright spell work surrounding it. One of the girls looked a little like

185

Frederica. Could that be her?

The scene changed again and a window popped up in the lower left hand corner with an attractive looking man who started blabbing about a recap. Honey half-listened while she closely watched the video now playing in the main window. Frederica was wandering around the library, touching the occasional book. Philomena Lambert walked into the shot and gestured toward the crystal on the table that couldn't be seen until the camera panned out. The two were clearly talking, but the sound wasn't part of the recording, leaving Honey suspicious as to why Frederica had touched the crystal or if she had ever touched it at all. Honey wouldn't put it past Philomena to doctor a video. The moment Frederica's finger landed on the tip of the crystal – again, it was impossible to tell if it was hers since the camera zoomed in to only show a finger touching the crystal and not who it belonged to – the crystal flashed and the finger disappeared. The next scene showed the crystal and the library as they were now and a portal opening in the middle of the bookshelves opposite the fireplace. Mr. Felix ran out, but he only managed a single step before a bright light zapped him and he fell where he lay now.

He hadn't even lasted a second. That didn't give her much time to do …what? She was almost 100% sure the crystal was a distraction. Philomena knew she could see spells, so why would she lie? Was it possible she *hadn't* figured out Honey was the girl in blue who had visited the school last spring? No, it was more likely she didn't think Honey would look before she leaped. The zap trap had a good chance of working, and if it had, Philomena's school would get credit for Honey's capture and that would be the end of it. On the other hand, if Honey did make it to the crystal and tried to break the curse, nothing would happen, proving she was a fraud.

Why have the picture there at all then?

Honey tried to imagine herself as Philomena. The spell-woman had already shown herself to be very crafty and likely held a grudge from Honey's last visit. The picture must be another trap of some kind. Maybe it would suck her in too or maybe Philomena wanted her to break it, although Honey guessed it wouldn't be because it did anything good.

She needed time to examine the picture and the spell but Philomena certainly wouldn't give it to her. No matter. She'd pop in, plant tethers on the Mr. Felix and the portrait, then pop out. Scratch that. Touching the picture would probably trap her too. She'd take the entire fireplace. It would serve Philomena right if it made the whole place fall down.

First though, research. There should be something in the library about magical portraits. She backed out of the group of students and slipped inside the library. Steering well clear of the line at the front desk, she headed for the section on enchanted objects. She'd never seen, nor had the section probably ever been so crowded. Half of the books were off the shelves and spread open on the tables. The only book left on the top shelf of the Magical Items section was a book titled '*Accursed Art*'. She pulled it off the shelf, then walked to the empty necromancy section and started to read.

"*Honey. Mr. Felix…*" Brayton sent fifteen minutes later.

"*I know. I saw.*"

"*New plan?*"

"*I'll tell you when I get there. Have Walter bring you a portal.*"

"*Still?*"

"*Yeah. Mr. Felix is not dead. He's in stasis, plus he wasn't wearing one of my shield bands. The spell won't be able to touch me.*"

"*Know how?*"

"*I can see the magic. Use your eye on the video. It's not a normal video, it's magic.*" She looked at her watch. "*Will you be at the station in twenty?*"

"*Fast to.*"

"*Thirty?*"

"*Too fast moving.*"

"*You think I'm moving too fast?*"

"*Yes.*"

"*The slower I go, the more likely it is someone will prepare an even bigger trap for me. I've got this Brayton. It's still a grab and go. I'll take my time once we're somewhere safe, so make sure wherever you decide on is safe.*"

"*Pressure no,*" he grumbled.

"*You know what, it doesn't even have to be in front of the cameras. Rescuing the Felixes is more important than people seeing it done.*"

"*See need.*"

"*My magic might make it impossible to record. I could just zap everything to the shed where my bike was stored.*"

"*Give two hours. Slow Walter.*"

"*Right, they have a long drive. Text him and tell him to be alone with the portal in five minutes and I'll pick it up.*"

"*Spies.*"

"*Then write it in code. How about 'Silver gift sticky situation in five.'*"

"*Obvious. May. Not. Read. In. Time.*"

"*You're right. Text them all, well, not Liam, I can't go to him,*" *and see which one responds, then tell them to find a quiet place."*

"Weird."

"Fine, say whatever you want, just tell me who to go to once they're ready."

"Then me?"

She checked her watch again. *"In nineteen minutes."*

"Impossible you are."

"Eighteen now Yoda."

"Can I sit here?" The student who'd called Mr. Felix stupid smiled down at her with three books in his hands.

She quite obviously glanced at the two empty tables on either side of her before shrugging. "Sure."

"This one has the best light. Which book did you find?"

She lifted the cover and showed him. He made a face. "That's worse than mine."

She glanced back toward the crowd in the magical artifact section. "Why is everyone so interested in the crystal?"

"Why are you so interested?" he shot back.

"I'm not."

"You don't care that some girl is trapped inside and might die if someone doesn't help her?"

"Are you going to try and help her?"

"I'm not a curse breaker, just curious is all. Besides, they canceled my magic class so we could watch."

"Really?"

"Yeah. This hybrid has been terrorizing everyone for months. Maybe now she'll finally be captured and on live TV too."

"Terrorizing?" Since when?

"Yeah. Don't you watch the news?"

189

"No, not usually." What lies had they been telling about her?

"You should."

"What has she done that's so terrible?"

"There was that bus crash full of children. Two of them died."

"Was she driving?"

"No, but it was due to the curse that they were hurt."

"Don't bus accidents happen occasionally anyway, just like all car accidents?"

"Not to witches. Then there was the mall shooting."

"What mall?" Was that why Frederica's cousin was no longer selling magic slates? Had she been killed?

"Somewhere in Missouri, but he only shot witches."

"Was he a witch?"

"Well, yeah, but that's not the point."

"You're not convincing me."

"What about the wolves?"

"What about the wolves," she asked.

"That Brayton kid. He lost an eye and then got his brain scrambled. Bad luck and his is worse because he knows her directly. If she cared for her friends she'd turn herself in so things like that wouldn't happen."

She just barely refrained from slamming her hands down on the table.

"Things like that happen because people like you make them happen, not because of the curse. People like you *are* the curse."

"Me? I haven't done anything."

"Exactly. Why are you satisfied with being under a curse? Why aren't you fighting it? Why aren't you insisting that the people still holding pieces of the curse destroy them? Once all the pieces are destroyed the curse won't exist and it won't matter if she's a hybrid or not."

"Witches and wolves together is unnatural."

"What, you're afraid that without the curse all witches and wolves will suddenly start falling for one another? Removing the curse doesn't mean they have to get together, but it will take away the major reason some fear becoming friends and it will certainly make a difference to the hybrid and her friends and family. She'll be able to have a normal life and pursue her dreams just like everyone else."

"She doesn't deserve it."

"Really? Why?"

"Because she's been hiding all this time while everyone else is suffering."

"You don't think she's suffering? You don't think she's not tired of running and sleeping out in the cold and always looking over her shoulder, afraid to even go in any store to buy food because someone might recognize her? You think you could do that – go for weeks on end without talking to anyone and eating as little food as possible so you have enough money to survive."

"You don't get it. If she'd just turn herself in, she wouldn't have to live like that. They'd put her out of her misery and we'd all go on with our lives. She's stressing out everyone for no reason."

Honey was so mad she had to whisper to keep from yelling. "She's a curse breaker. The first one in centuries. This is your chance and everyone else's chance to get out from under a horrible curse that's caused thousands of deaths not just due to killing of hybrids and their parents, but also because of the animosity it has encouraged between wolves and witches. You'd rather just kill her and continue to live like that?"

"She's just one girl. Besides, she hasn't really done anything to break the curse."

"Really?!"

"Honey. Walter. Ready."

She stood, nearly knocking her chair over in the process. "You're lucky I have to go see a man about a portal, idiot."

She threw herself into the nether and popped out a moment later in a closet with Walter.

"Whoa, giving off some strong angry vibes there Luna."

She grabbed the unbuttoned edges of Walter's flannel shirt and shook him. "Do you think I should just turn myself in? Do you think I'm stupid for wanting to help people? If they don't care about the curse, why should I?"

"Hey, no," he pulled her into a hug. "You're not stupid. They've just lived with it so long, they don't realize how evil it is. You're doing the right thing."

She leaned against his shoulder and let out a long sigh. "I'm just…I'm so tired. I just want to go to school and be normal."

"I know."

He didn't say anything else, just held her. It was exactly what she needed. She pushed away after a few minutes and gave him a nod. "Thank you."

"My pleasure, Luna Honey."

She wrinkled her nose at him. "That's just, no."

"Doesn't Brayton call you that?"

"He hasn't yet."

"Do you want him to?"

"I don't know," she admitted. "I like him as a friend, and he is a good kisser, but," she sighed.

Walter pulled her close again and rested his chin on her head. "It's a lot to wrap your head around. It's only been a couple of weeks. Give it time. Good, strong relationships take a while to build. I think you and Brayton have promise."

"It would have been easier if I could have picked you."

"Me?"

She nodded. "You're already my best friend and I care for you, a lot. I should have chosen you as my alpha."

"I'm not an alpha though, and I think, for you to fulfill your role, which I am convinced you were selected for by some higher power, you need an alpha. You need Brayton."

"But I like you."

He sighed and squeezed her tighter. "I like you too Honey."

"Honey, where are you? Did you get the portal? Are you coming?"

She stepped out of Walter's hug. "He's calling me. Do you have the portal?"

"Yeah. Here." He pressed something in her hand. "Good luck."

"Thank you."

"No, thank you Honey, for doing this for everyone."

"You going to watch?"

"I wouldn't miss it."

She gave him another smile and threw herself back into the nether again.

34

BRAYTON – BEFORE 10 AM – INDIANA

His favorite pair of lips brushed against his, then vanished. She smelled like Walter, like covered in Walter. He must have hugged her. It made him jealous and sad at the same time. Would she ever spontaneously hug him like she did her friends?

"It get?"

She held up a little white shell. "Yep. Where are we?"

"Recognize don't?"

Someone flipped the lights, illuminating an indoor track and basketball courts.

"The wolf gym under the regular gym."

"Yep."

"Is that my grandmother?"

He'd never seen a more beautiful smile.

"Yep."

She didn't hear him. She was already half-way to the bleachers. Her grandmother barely had time to stand before Honey was throwing her arms around her.

"Honey! Goodness, I didn't recognize you in that getup."

"Oh! I forgot I was wearing it."

She tugged off her hat and wig then touched her skirt and made it disappear, revealing a pair of sweats. A second later, she had everything tucked into the backpack she'd magicked out of the air.

"Don't forget the frames," Grandma said.

"Right, and the contacts. Better?"

Her grandmother reached up and ran her fingers through Honey's short hair. "Yes. Your mother wanted to cut her hair short when she was your age. I never let her."

"I only did it to change my appearance."

Her grandmother pulled her into another hug. "I know. I've missed you."

"Why are you here? Did you take a look at Brayton?"

"Not yet, our appointment isn't for another hour. Brayton texted and asked me to come early just in case. I hope Mr. Felix is okay."

"The spell looks like a cocoon. I think he's just in stasis."

"Oh good. What about the crystal? Could you tell what kind of curse it is?"

"The crystal is a decoy. Frederica's stuck in the painting above the fireplace."

"Really?" Brayton asked behind her.

"Pretty sure. Look at it next time they show it. The magic on it is nearly blinding and one of the girls looks like Frederica."

"What's your plan Honey?" Grandpa asked. The short, forty-something man Grandpa had introduced as one of the best cameramen he'd ever met was by his side.

"I'm going to jump through a portal and grab things."

"You sure you'll be able to grab Mr. Felix and the picture and get them back through the portal in ten seconds? We only have one," Grandpa said.

"Actually, I just want to make it look like I took them out through the portal. I'm guessing Philomena will block the portal as soon as I'm through. Suggestions on how to

195

do that?"

"Smoke grenade," Grandpa's friend said.

"I like it. Do you have one."

The man looked at Honey as if that was the stupidest question he'd ever heard, then said, "Of course. What color?"

"You have different colors?!" Honey squealed.

Brayton shook his head. Of course, she would get excited about colored smoke grenades. Maybe he could buy her some for her birthday.

"I do. What's your favorite color?"

"Blue."

"Good choice. I recommend both a dark and a light. It will be more dramatic. You can jump through the portal holding them."

"I prefer to keep my hands free."

"Wise. We can just toss them in then."

"Who are you?" she asked.

He stuck out his hand. "Abraham Maldonado, action cinematographer, and you are the infamous Honey Smith."

"I prefer just Honey, but it's nice to meet you, as long as you aren't going to try and kill me or something equally egregious."

He snort-smiled and his eyes flicked to her forehead. "No. I would never do that. Tell me, how do you plan on bringing Mr. Felix and his daughter here if the portal is closed?"

"There will be magic involved."

"Flashy magic?"

"More like now you see it, now you don't, except the other way around. I promise you an interesting surprise though."

"A surprise. I like that. Will there be an explosion?"

"I sincerely hope not."

"That's too bad. Maybe the smoke bomb will explode. That happened to me once."

"And you still have all your fingers?"

"Most of them." He wiggled a hand to show half of one finger was missing.

"Lucky."

"Yes," the man nodded. "I just need a few minutes to finish setting up."

A few minutes turned into twenty, but the center of the floor was now protected with old mats and there was a mobile wall Brayton could use for the portal on the edge of the mats. Abraham angled the wall to the camera in such a way that it would look like Honey was stepping out of the portal even though she would be using a tether attached to the wall to get back.

"You two ready?" Abraham finally asked.

Brayton looked back at Honey who was standing in the middle of the mat. She took a deep breath, then released it with a nod.

"Ready. Light 'em up."

Brayton's grandparents ripped the pins off the smoke grenades and held them out to the side. Grandma's eyes were sparkling and she had a big grin on her face, like she enjoyed throwing grenades. Huh.

Honey nudged him. "Brayton, open the portal."

Oops. He obediently pictured the wall next to the fireplace like Honey had instructed.

"Toss them through," Honey said.

Grandma tossed her canister through like she was

tossing a beanbag. Grandpa, on the other hand, flung his canister as hard as he could.

"Perfect," Abraham said from where he was watching the live footage Philomena was still streaming on a tablet. "We have great smoke coverage. Go Honey."

Brayton couldn't see anything through the portal except billowing blue smoke, but less than five seconds later, Honey popped into existence beside his portal, and a moment later, Mr. Felix was in her arms. She ran forward and laid him in the center of the mat. While Abraham zoomed in on Mr. Felix's face, Honey touched the ground and suddenly there was an entire fireplace, complete with a chimney and a fire in the middle of the gym.

Meanwhile Mrs. Wixx had stepped onto the mat and dropped to her knees by Mr. Felix's side. "Honey, can you remove the spell?"

"Sure Grandma."

Brayton blinked twice, curious to see what her magic looked like. All he saw was a bright light where the tip of her claw met the glowing spell surrounding Mr. Felix. She ran her claw from the top of Mr. Felix's head all the way to his shoes. The spell fell open like a peanut shell that vanished when it hit the ground. Mr. Felix gasped and his eyes flew open.

"Frederica?"

Mrs. Wixx put her hand on his chest. "Stay still for a bit. You just came out from under a spell. Honey's here. She'll rescue your daughter."

"Again."

"Again," Mrs. Wixx agreed.

"Why?" Brayton waved his hand up and down at the fireplace, certain if anyone was watching, they'd want to know too.

"Why did I bring the entire fireplace here?"

He nodded.

"I wasn't sure how the picture spell worked and I didn't want to touch it until I'd had a good look at it," Honey said, "and a good sniff." She put her nose up close and held it there a few minutes. "I smell iron and cold and stone, like a prison, but I also smell," she sniffed, then cocked her head. "Gun powder, but maybe that's from the smoke grenades."

Brayton felt a breeze and the smoke still lingering from the grenades drifted toward the other end of the gym.

"Nope, it's coming from the spell. Oh, I get it. If I try to destroy the curse, it will explode, killing me and likely everyone inside. I have to get them out first."

"Them?" Brayton asked.

Honey nodded. "Yes, the younger Ms. Lambert is in there too. She's the other girl in the picture."

"How did you know they weren't in the crystal?" Mr. Felix asked from the floor.

"It didn't have enough magic," Honey answered, frowning at the picture.

"Wrong what?" Brayton asked.

"I need a key."

"A special key or will any key do?" Grandpa asked.

"Any key I think."

"Try this."

Grandpa reached under his collar and produced the old skeleton key he'd worn around his neck as long as Brayton had known him.

Honey took it from him with a grin. "Perfect."

199

She pressed her thumb against one of her clawed fingers, releasing the smell of blood, then rubbed her thumb against the key.

"Here goes nothing."

All Brayton could see was a glow around the picture, but it must have looked like something else to Honey, because she inserted the key into the glow in a very specific spot and turned it, then stepped back. The glow expanded. At the same time, the two girls in the painting grew and swelled to become three dimensional, then finally tumbled out of the picture and onto the floor.

"Frederica!" Mr. Felix called from where he was now sitting, supported by a smiling Mrs. Wixx.

"Dad!"

Frederica rushed into her dad's arms.

Honey moved to stand in front of the other girl from the portrait while she pushed herself up.

"You okay?"

"Honey Smith."

Brayton noticed the girl's hand was poised like she was about to put it in her pocket but it wasn't moving.

"Yep, in the flesh. Do you recognize me?" Honey walked around the girl, grabbed her under the armpits, and pulled her up. The girl's hand still didn't move.

"Not really. It was a good disguise."

"Thank you, and I truly am sorry I couldn't tell you who I was that day. I hope you understand why now."

"I do."

"Why don't you have a seat over there out of the way. We can talk later. I have spell to destroy," Honey said, pointing toward the bleachers.

"You froze my arms, didn't you."

"Yep. I also disabled the charms in your pocket. Alpha Braxton, you should remove that ugly ring she's wearing on her index finger. I suspect it contains poison."

"Poison?" Brayton asked.

"I'm pretty sure she's just following Philomena's instructions," Honey said casually. "You guys should all back away. I think our cameraman might get his explosion after all."

"How far?" Grandpa asked.

"I'd clear the mats."

"About you what?" Brayton asked.

"I'll move fast."

She was seriously going to give him an anxiety attack.

Honey grabbed Brayton's shoulders, turned him toward his grandpa, and gave him a little push. "I'll be fine Brayton. Go stand by Alpha Braxton."

Reluctantly, he did as she asked. Grandpa gave him an empathetic little smile and put his arm around Brayton's shoulders. It was nice, but there was no way Grandma had ever caused Grandpa as much grief as Honey did him.

Honey looked around to make sure everyone was clear, put her hands in front of the picture like she was grabbing two bars and ripped them apart.

There was a loud boom. Bricks shot everywhere. Worse was the thick, choking dust that billowed out, hiding everything on the mat.

"Honey? Honey where is?" Brayton asked desperately, pushing away from Grandpa to search the dust cloud. Was she on the ground? Was she bleeding? There was no way she could have avoided those bricks. The dust was worse than the smoke grenades.

He'd only walked a few steps into the cloud when

201

warm lips landed on his. He grabbed his Honey before she could escape again.

"Never. Again."

"I told you I'd be okay."

He planted a kiss on her so she couldn't say anything else to make him anxious.

"Oh my gosh, that's my mom's sweater," the girl who'd planned to kill Honey said from the side of the mat where Grandpa was still keeping an eye on her.

"Where's your mom's sweater?" Honey asked the other girl while pushing herself out of his arms.

"Inside the fireplace. That..that was her favorite sweater. She wore it all the time."

For the first time, Brayton took a good look at what was left of the fireplace and the chimney. Despite the huge billowing cloud of dust and what had seemed like a truck-full of flying bricks, there was a lot left. The explosion had only knocked a hole in the chimney nearly the exact size and location of the cursed painting, but what it revealed was grim. Three fully clothed skeletons, and maybe more, were stuffed together inside the bricks.

"When did she disappear?" Honey asked.

"Eight years ago. I was twelve. She just vanished one day."

"Who else went missing?"

"Her mom, my grandmother, when my mom was fifteen. I don't know who else."

"Your great-grandmother," Mrs. Wixx said. It happened when I was a little girl. I remember because she just vanished but there was no explanation. Everyone liked her, at least that was my impression."

"But who would do this?" the girl asked.

"I'll give you a hint," Honey huffed. "It starts with a 'P'"

"Aunt Philomena? No, she would never."

"Who else has been around long enough to have killed your great-grandmother?"

"But why?"

"Maybe they did something she didn't agree with," Honey suggested, "and she decided it was time for the next generation to take over."

"She *is* a little old-fashioned," the young woman admitted, "but she's not a murderer."

"Honey," Grandpa interrupted, "visitors on the way. You best go."

"You guys will be okay? I could get you out of here too."

"We'll be fine," Grandpa said.

"I would love to go with you," Mrs. Wixx said, touching Honey's cheek, "but I would just slow you down." She pulled her into a tight hug.

"Honey," Mr. Felix said behind Mrs. Wixx, "Thanks for saving my daughter again."

"Glad I could help."

Brayton could hear the sirens now.

"Oh, I should send the fireplace back," Honey said, "but.."

"No," the girl said. "Aunt Philomena is there and the bodies...my mom..."

"I'm sorry I messed up your school," Honey said.

"That can be fixed. Dealing with Aunt Philomena on the other hand, will be a challenge. She doesn't like to lose."

"I might have some artifacts that will help," Mrs. Wixx

said. "I cannot break spells like Honey, but a lot of my ancestors could." She sent Brayton a sly wink.

"I meant it's going to be difficult to calm her down, not that I want to destroy her," the would-be murderer said.

"I think," Mr. Felix interrupted, "that you've had a shock, a very big one, and you need some time to let things sink in. We are also only speculating right now that it was your Aunt Philomena and have no proof. We have plenty of time to discuss that, but Honey, you need to go."

"Okay."

"Wait!" Brayton grabbed her arm and pulled her into a tight hug. "Amazing," he whispered into her ear. "I'll. Ask. About. Curse."

"Thank you, Brayton."

She backed out of his arms and pressed something into his hand, then she was gone, again.

"Mr. Felix," Grandpa said at the same time the doors on opposite sides of the gym crashed open. "Are you up to another trip to Texas? I have a feeling the Enforcers are going to be quite busy for a while. We should get out of their way."

"Indeed," Mr. Felix said, climbing to his feet, "and I know a great place where we can have some brunch."

The floor started to waver in front of him. "Quickly everyone."

35

BRAYTON – STILL MORNING – TEXAS

The key. That's what she'd pressed into his hand. The brown/gray metal was now streaked with burgundy.

"I believe the school is this way," Mr. Felix said, turning to his left. "As is that restaurant I mentioned."

"I need to get back to the school," Ms. Lambert said.

"Then that is where we shall go."

"Is there anyone else there at the moment Mistress Lambert?" Mrs. Wixx asked, falling into step beside her and in front of Brayton.

"Call me Vera and no. All the students are home on Thanksgiving break."

"Good, then we don't have to worry about anyone else being trapped," Mr. Felix said.

"Unless the Enforcers are on the grounds," Grandpa said behind Brayton.

"I doubt my aunt will have allowed them inside," Vera said.

"What do you plan to do?" Mrs. Wixx asked.

"I will ask Aunt Philomena if she killed my mother."

"Can you trust her not to lie?" Grandpa asked.

"She cannot lie, only omit."

"Will you be able to film a spell person?" Grandpa asked the cameraman who was following them with a heavy-looking camera on one shoulder and a bag of equipment on the other.

"If I use my special camera."

Grandma asked the question Brayton was wondering. "Did you use it to film Honey?"

"I did, but the camera is not digital so I couldn't broadcast it live."

"What will you do if your aunt admits to harming your mother?" Frederica asked Vera over her shoulder.

"I will destroy her," Vera said firmly.

"Do you have a way to do that?" Mrs. Wixx asked gently.

"I do."

Vera's voice didn't waiver but Brayton could smell her angst.

"What about your father? Perhaps he could help," Grandma said kindly.

"I never knew my father. He disappeared shortly after I was born. Aunt said he was a useless lout good only for sperm donation. No," she said when the silence dragged on. "He wasn't killed. He abandoned us."

"What about your mother's father? Is he still alive," Mrs. Wixx asked.

"No. He went to fight in the war and never came back."

"That's really sad," Frederica said after another long period of silence.

Brayton looked behind him and caught Grandpa's eye. Grandpa suspected they'd find more skeletons too.

"Key?" Brayton said, offering the key to Grandpa to change the subject.

"Keep it."

"From where?" Brayton asked, immediately putting the cord that held the key over his own neck.

"The day you were born, I found this key in a parking lot. A passing witch told me I should keep it with me and that my grandson's Luna would find it helpful someday. That was before anyone knew you were a boy."

"You listened to a witch?" Vera asked in surprise.

"I have nothing against witches as long as they don't try to use their magic on me."

Mr. Felix led them up a flight of stairs and onto a wide street. After a couple of blocks, he turned onto a smaller street with older buildings and shaded sidewalks. Numerous vehicles with flashing lights were in front of a large house half-way down the block.

"Wait Mr. Felix," Grandpa said. "I think you and Frederica and Mrs. Wixx should stay here. Nancy, would you mind staying with them in case we need to communicate?"

Grandma patted Grandpa's cheek. "Nice try dear, but I'm sure they can operate a phone just as well as I can."

"Nancy."

"Oh, all right, but if you get in trouble, I'm coming in."

Grandpa kissed her cheek. "I'm counting on it. Brayton, why don't you give Vera one of those shield charms. Abe, you need one?"

"Nope, I'm good."

"Vera, take this too," Mr. Felix said, offering her something in his hand.

"What is it?"

"Portastone. Legally, I can't use stone, but I'm not selling it and this is an emergency. All you have to do is throw it on the ground and it will immediately form a portal back to me. I'll hold it open as long as it's needed."

"Thank you."

"All right Vera, lead on," Grandpa said.

"You might as well stay here too," the girl said, chewing on her lip. "The protection spell over the grounds won't let wolves in."

"I'm going to make sure the Enforcers let you through and let Abe film things. Brayton is my backup."

"Brayton may be able to take down the spell if you get in trouble," Mrs. Wixx added. "Honey left him a gift."

Brayton wondered if anyone else knew what she was talking about.

Mrs. Wixx smiled at his confusion, then wiggled her finger at him so he'd lean down to where she could whisper in his ear. "A key with the blood of a curse breaker will open any spell and break weak curses, future grandson?"

He straightened to look into her kind blue eyes and nodded. "Hope I."

"Mmm," she put her hand on his cheek and he felt her magic wash through his head. "You're a good boy Brayton. She could do much worse." She took her hand away. "That should jump start the detangling process."

"You thank."

The road in front of the museum/school was completely blocked off. A curvy woman with a young face and iron gray hair stepped forward when Grandpa reached for the caution tape.

"You're either awfully brave or awfully stupid to show your face here," the woman said.

"Why do you say that?" Grandpa asked.

The woman waved to a van where Brayton could just see some computer monitors through the partially open sliding door. "You are now a known associate of the hydrid."

"I was already a known associate of the hybrid seeing as how she was previously in my pack." Grandpa thrust his hand out. "I'm Alpha Braxton Mooney. It's nice to meet you Ms…"

The woman put her much smaller hand in his. "Captain Marilla LeDoux, but now you're on film telling her to leave."

"We can discuss that later. For now, we have a bigger problem." He gestured for Vera to step forward. "I bring the owner. You no doubt saw the skeletons which we believe are her relatives. She's the only one who can communicate with the spell that may be responsible. I assume that's why you guys are here, to investigate the murders?"

The woman snorted and shook her head. "Sure, we can go with that. Why don't you and your grandson find yourselves seats in that comfortable looking van over there," she pointed to a black van with bars on the back window. Brayton could see a glow around it which was either a protection spell or a magic dampening spell.

"We'll pass. We're here to film the interaction and provide protection if needed," Grandpa said.

"You're wolves. You won't even get on the property."

"Maybe Ms. Lambert doesn't need to be on the property. Ms. Lambert, can you speak to your Aunt from here?"

"The front gate will be best."

Captain LeDoux jerked her chin toward the nearly solid line of enforcers now standing along the caution tape. "Let them through."

"Have any of your non-wolf people been able to get on the property?" Grandpa asked after they'd all ducked under the tape.

"Not since that hybrid pulled the fireplace out of the building," Captain LeDoux replied. "Did she use some kind of portal charm or a transmutation spell?"

"I don't know. Just to make it clear, today is the first time I've seen or spoken to Honey since last spring. That was before she 'came out' as it were."

"Uh-huh. After you."

The crowd of enforcers moved aside just enough to clear a path to the gate. Brayton should have felt protected since he was in line between his grandpa and Abraham, but the stench of magic from all the witches and the huge magical dome he could see surrounding the house started pushing down on him. He couldn't breathe.

"Brayton, you okay?"

Brayton registered the voice and the hand on his shoulder as Abraham's, but it was too much. He punched it off with a growl.

"Brayton, Brayton, whoa buddy," Grandpa said. "Captain, can you have your people back up please? It's okay Brayton. Look at me. Deep breaths. Captain, back up your people please. He's had a rough week. I think the smell of magic is setting him off. This is what happens when witches torture a wolf. He needs space and fresh air. Dammit, put that away! He's not going to hurt you. He just needs space."

Brayton closed his eyes. He could feel every single person around him, crowding him, touching him, that witch touching him, Damien touching him. He clenched his fists and yelled.

"BACK. OFF!"

The voices around him ceased. Fresh air bathed his face. The smell of magic, while still there, faded as did the horrible suffocating feeling. He took a couple of breaths of fresh air and opened his eyes. He was standing in the middle of the street alone. The enforcers that had been too close were now standing around the vans and vehicles parked on the side of the road and quite obviously not looking at him.

"You better," his grandpa asked from twenty feet away.

"Yeah."

"Come over here then while Vera talks to her aunt. She said as long as we stay on the sidewalk, we should be safe. Her aunt's spell doesn't extend past the property line."

"What was that?" Captain LeDoux asked from even farther away than Grandpa.

"That was my grandson's alpha power." Grandpa's eyes twinkled with amusement when he turned back to Brayton. "Apparently you're so strong you can even command witches."

"Impossible," the captain hissed under her breath.

Grandpa shaded his eyes and looked up the street. "I think some of the wolves are still backing away. Speaking of, you think you can release Abraham so he can get the camera set up?"

"Sure." Brayton exhaled out a 'stand down' command.

A moment later, Abraham marched across the street towing his camera and muttering under his breath, something about fat flying pigs mixed in with some not-so-polite words. He quickly set up two cameras, one that

211

looked like an old-fashioned movie camera complete with reels of film, and a smaller one with a big microphone sticking out the front of it. He also had a small one on his head.

"Ready."

Vera nodded and stepped right in front of the gate. "Aunt Philomena, I need to talk to you. Come to me."

A kind-looking older woman materialized just inside the gate. "There you are dear. I've been looking for you. That hybrid stole our chimney."

"Why did you trap me inside the picture?" Vera demanded.

"To keep you safe. I would've let you out once I caught the hybrid," the woman-spell said innocently.

"Like you did my mother?" Vera accused.

"Surely you don't think I had anything to do with that?"

"You knew she was there?"

"Yes."

"And you didn't tell me?"

"It wouldn't have done any good," the woman-spell said gently.

"You know everything that happens in the school. Who killed my mother," Vera asked. Her voice was starting to mellow out like she believed it could be someone other than her aunt.

"No one killed her, dear. She died of natural causes."

"What cause? What, exactly killed her?"

"I'm not a doctor. I don't know exactly."

"Did you trap my mother in the picture?"

"No."

"Was she trapped in the picture?"

"Yes."

"Who trapped her?" Vera asked.

"She trapped herself."

"Did you arrange for her to come in contact with the picture so that she would get trapped?" Grandpa intervened.

The spell-woman wrinkled her nose. "I don't converse with animals. Vera, why are you in the company of these beasts?"

"Answer the question Aunt. Did you arrange for my mother to accidentally or on purpose trap herself in the picture?"

"I didn't push her, if that's what you're asking."

"It is not and you know it isn't. Did she ever get out of the picture once she was trapped?"

"No."

"She died in the picture?"

"Yes."

"How is that a natural cause? That's a magical cause!"

"No. She may have been magically trapped, but it wasn't magic that killed her."

"She starved," Captain LeDoux stated bluntly.

"Yes," the spell-woman agreed.

"You let my mother starve?!" Vera cried out.

"She didn't feel a thing," the spell-woman said. "You were in the picture. Do you remember anything?"

"That's not the point!"

"Calm down child. You're embarrassing yourself."

"How many other people have you allowed to die inside the picture?" Vera demanded.

"Mmm, it's been a while since I counted. Twenty-three that I know of."

"Twenty-three," Vera said weakly. "My dad?"

"Yes, he was one."

"My grandpa?"

"Yes and his meddling sister."

Vera's shoulders sagged, "Aunt Philomena, how could you? They were my family."

"Trust me, you're not missing anything. They were my family too, remember."

"What happened to all the bodies," Captain LeDoux asked.

"The picture takes care of that."

"I've seen an enchanted item like that before," a male enforcer on the other side of the captain said. "After the enchantment pulls as much magical energy as it can from its victim, it deposits the body into whatever it's hanging on, usually the wall, and resets as a blank canvas. The blankness where a loved one was attracts the next victim."

"That's awful," Vera said. "Why did we even have something like that?"

"It was made before my time," the spell-woman said.

"Do you have any other items in the house that you've used to get rid of pesky relatives or other people?" the captain asked.

"I'm not programmed to respond to you."

"Aunt Philomena, answer the question," Vera demanded.

"There's a poisonous cup but I only used that once to get rid of a pesky suitor. Poison is too messy. And the wards, of course, which can kill a wolf if I turn them up to full power, but then more of them come snooping around. I only use that on rogues."

"Who did you kill with the cup?" Vera asked.

"Who do you think?"

"Michael?" Vera squeaked, "You killed Michael?"

"I told you I would find someone suitable for you."

"Michael was perfect!"

The spell-woman scoffed. "You have more power in one pinky than he ever dreamed of having. We are Lamberts. We only marry the best or we don't marry at all."

"Which is why there are so few of us alive now," Vera stormed.

"I think it's more likely because she killed them all," the captain commented. "Why though? Why did you kill off your family? Why did you kill Vera's parents?"

"She didn't need them. She had me. Because of my multi-generational experience, I am an infinitely better parent."

"I hate to say this, but I think something has gone seriously wrong with your aunt's spell," Grandpa said.

"Yes," Vera said sadly.

Tears were starting to carve rivers down her cheeks but, Brayton noted as he looked around at all the people watching, she didn't have a single friend or family member to comfort her. Had the stupid spell killed her friends too? Was no one going to comfort her? She was just like Honey, all alone. He hated to see girls, or anyone, cry.

He walked over to her and squeezed her shoulder. "Alone not you."

She looked up at him with her tears streaming and he had to do something. He put his arm around her shoulders and pulled her into a hug. "Everyone sometimes a hug needs. Witches even."

She nodded and sniffed and probably dripped all over

his shirt, but he didn't let it bother him.

"Vera! Get away from that wolf! Do you want to curse our line with a hybrid?"

The witch in his arms pushed away from him and angrily swiped the tears off her cheeks with both hands. "It was just a hug, aunt. Do you know how long it's been since I had a good hug? Michael. Michael was the last person to give me a hug and you killed him."

"No. He killed himself when he drank from the poisonous cup."

"But you gave it to him. Did he know it was poisonous?"

"I don't know."

"Aunt, your services are no longer needed. Shut yourself down."

"Now dear, don't be hasty. You've had a bit of a shock, but nothing has changed. I'm the same, you're the same. Just forget about it and move on."

"I'm detecting a spike in the magical signature," a man yelled from a van.

"She's messing with my cameras," Abraham said.

"She's trying to lay a forget-it spell on us too," a woman enforcer said.

"Stop it, Aunt. That won't work. I gave you direct command. Since I am now old enough to be the matron of this school you must obey me. Shut yourself down."

"You need me dear."

"Shut yourself down. Now."

"I cannot follow that order since it would be detrimental to the school."

"There is no school, not now, not with all those dead people in the walls. I'm going to rebuild somewhere else.

216

The house will be torn down."

"Vera, you are going to walk away from the wolves and come into the house and have some tea where we will discuss this rationally."

"The magic is spiking again," the man in the van warned.

"No, aunt. Shut down, now. You've destroyed the school. No one will want to stay here anymore."

"I protected the school. I will keep protecting the school. The bodies have never bothered anyone. They will all forget. Come inside."

"Drop the wards, Aunt."

"With all those wolves out there? Are you daft? Come inside where I can protect you."

"Poison me you mean. Shut down!"

"You have no power over me. I fixed the weakness in my spell a long time ago. Now come inside."

"Captain, is there anyone here who can breach the wards?" Grandpa asked.

"What do you think we've been trying to do since the challenge was placed?"

"Wards are getting stronger," the man in the van called.

Brayton didn't need the notice. He could smell, feel, and see the power. He pulled the key from around his neck.

"Brayton," Grandpa said sharply.

"Touch won't," Brayton said. "Just key."

The ward looked like a big, upside-down glowing bowl. He couldn't discern any features, let alone keyholes, but it made sense to try where the gate was. He poked the key into the glow and turned.

Brayton wasn't sure what he expected, but after the explosion Honey caused when she broke the curse on the picture, he thought there would be a little more action when he turned the key. Maybe there was. All he saw was the glow from the wards disappear and the glare the spell-woman shot at him right before she popped out of existence.

"Ward down! Ward down!" the man in the van yelled in unbridled excitement.

"Let's move people," Captain LeDoux yelled. "We need that spell contained before she murders anyone else. Ms. Lambert, where does the source of your aunt's power reside?"

"I'm not sure. Maybe the library or perhaps the small office right off the library. It belonged to my real Aunt Philomena at one time."

"All right. You folks stay here." Her eyes dropped to the key in Brayton's hand. "We might need that."

"That was gifted specifically to Brayton," Grandpa said before Brayton could think of a suitable way to tell her she wasn't getting it. "I'm not sure it's safe for anyone else to wield."

"Hmm. Well, don't go anywhere."

"Captain." The van man had poked his head out of the van but was still looking back inside. "You're going to want to see this. The whole yard is rigged with magical traps and explosions. You step one toe off the sidewalk and I can't even guess what will happen. Oh, and part of the sidewalk is lighting up too."

"STOP!" the captain yelled. "Do not step onto the property yet! Ms. Lambert, with me," the captain demanded before stalking to the van.

"Oh great," Abe grumbled.

Brayton turned to see what Abe's problem was just as a pink news van with a couple of dishes on top lurched to a halt next to the caution tape. A voluptuous woman with perfectly styled brown hair, blindingly white teeth, and a well-fitted dress stepped out of the van, somehow not stumbling in her four-inch heels. She marched up to the tape and surveyed the scene beyond it. A couple of men tumbled out of the van behind her, one sporting a large camera on his shoulder. The woman's gaze was cool and searching until it fell on Abe, then her face split into a predatory grin that was as frightening as it was beautiful.

"That who's?" Brayton asked.

"My worst nightmare," Abe replied when she ducked under the tape and marched purposely in his direction.

"Abe – Abraham, I see you've saved me a spot."

"This is my story Sandra."

Her eyes lifted pointedly to the camera strapped to his forehead, then to the ancient one still recording.

"Right."

She turned her back on him and started directing her own cameraman where to stand.

"Do you mind if I move this?" she asked Abe even while she bent like she was going to lift his ancient camera.

"If you don't mind losing your body parts. I've had it spelled since the last time we met."

"It's in my shot."

"I guess it's not your shot then."

She frowned and looked around, then moved to stand directly in front of Brayton. "You. Move."

Like he would obey a command from a stranger, and a witch at that.

"Do you know who I am?"

She did look a little familiar, but he just raised an eyebrow.

"Sandra Soulton of WTV news. *The* leading on-the-scene reporter for all that is magical."

A few nicely cutting remarks ran through his head, but unfortunately they wouldn't survive his tongue.

"You wolves are all the same," she huffed. "No appreciation for quality reporting. Come Goran, we can get a better shot in front of the gate."

The scrawny witch with the large camera obediently followed her. She stopped right smack in front of the gate despite the enforcers milling around and turned to face the camera. The scrawny guy handed her a pink microphone. She turned it on, looked up at the camera, and smiled. Like magic, which it might have been, her features transformed from shrewd go-getter to beautiful neighbor next-door.

Now he recognized her.

"I'm here in front of the Opal Lambert School for Witches and Wizards where the spell version of Philomena Lambert has just admitted to contributing to the deaths of at least twenty-three people, including the parents of the current twenty-one-year-old matron of the school, Vera Lambert. Enforcers are on the scene and are in discussion with the young Madame Lambert as to how to best contain and disable Philomena. Philomena is a powerful caregiver spell modified and maintained over several generations and has full control of the many protective measures placed on the house and grounds, some of which are deadly. Stay tuned here for further developments. This is Sandra Soulton, your go-to girl for breaking news."

"How know?" Brayton asked Abe who was literally grinding his teeth.

"Some sort of spell I'm sure. She's scooped every single story she's ever reported, generally from wolves."

"Spy spell."

"Probably."

Brayton took a closer look at Abe's equipment. He'd thought the little dobs of magic on the cameras were to protect them from other magic, but upon closer inspection, he realized they were magical spying ladybugs. He started casually running his hand with the ring over the dots.

"So, how have you been Abe?" the now gloating Sandra bounced back to join them. "I saw you had a new nature documentary on YouTube. Your three followers must be very excited."

"Keep it up Sandra. Someday your cheating is going to come back to bite you."

"I'm not cheating. I'm using the gifts I've been given."

She lifted her hands and wiggled her fingers. Little bug-shaped bits of magic flicked off her fingers and flew toward the camera he'd just cleaned. He hated cheaters. Brayton faced her directly, pulled up as much alpha power as he could, then put it all into one word.

"NO."

The witch flinched like he'd hit her and dropped her hands, then curled her nose at him. "I don't like your friend, Abe."

"Good." Abe leaned closer to Brayton while they watched the woman flounce away and asked, "What was that about?"

Brayton wiggled his fingers like she had. "Spy spells."

"Huh, I thought it was just a quirky thing she did." He looked at his equipment and sighed. "Guess I'm going to have to find a witch who can protect my equipment from spy spells. Stupid witches."

"I heard that," Captain LeDoux said behind him.

"Of course you did," Abe said under his breath.

"Carr, Duncan, you're up," the Captain called.

Two wolves in enforcer gear and loaded down with various weapons threaded their way through the other enforcers to stand at attention in front of her.

"Take a look at what Albert has on the screen, then come out here and see how many traps you can set off, particularly on the sidewalk."

"That might get loud," Grandpa commented.

"We've got sound dampers and look-away spells in place. Trust me, we've managed to hide things much larger than this. Who are you?" The captain looked past Brayton's grandpa where Sandra had appeared with her microphone angled to catch the conversation.

"Sandra Soulton. You've probably seen me on WTV. I'm their top reporter."

"You shouldn't be here. Someone get her and her cameraman out of here."

"*He's* here!" Sandra indicated Abe.

"He's…helping," the captain grimaced.

It was a blatant lie. Brayton again wondered how witches couldn't smell them.

"Helping with what?"

"Helping us keep costs down so we don't have to send anyone out to arrest him."

Sandra laughed, then put on her serious face and said

222

into the microphone, "Is this because of his friendship with the hybrid, Honey Smith?"

"You are interfering with Enforcer business Ms... Reporter. Please move yourself to the other side of the caution tape."

"Ready boss," one of the two wolves said. He was carrying something that looked an awful lot like a PVC potato cannon painted in camouflage.

The captain scowled at the gun. "That's what you're using?"

"If the spells are weight triggered we'll be able to see what we're up against."

"And maybe have some fries on the side," the other one joked.

The captain shook her head. "How long have you been carrying that around?"

"A while."

"Fire in the hole!" the other wolf called right before his buddy shot his gun.

"That's not...never mind," the captain muttered, shaking her head.

The potato shot out of the cannon faster than Brayton could follow it. Light flashed. Small pieces of potato bounced onto the grass in at least a ten-foot radius.

"Looks like we're having exploded potatoes instead," the second wolf said.

"Anything happen?" the captain called back to van man.

"Nope, all the spells are still in place."

"Damn, I was afraid of that," the captain said under her breath.

"What?" Brayton asked.

The wolf with the cannon answered. "Some spells are like landmines. Once they go off, they're gone. Other spells are like shielded bunkers with gun turrets. These are the gun turret kind."

Grandpa asked what Brayton was wondering. "How will you get past them?"

The second wolf pulled a big black gun out of the holster on his back. "Magic bullets. The shields don't work against normal bullets but normal bullets don't work against spells. We have bullets that are a mix of magic and lead. The lead will go through the shield and the magic payload will destroy the spell. They don't work on big wards, unfortunately, but they should work on small ones." He pulled a pair of glasses with a faint magic glow from the top of his head over his eyes. "You probably won't be able to see anything, but if it works, you might hear something."

The wolf was wrong. Brayton's ears were too irritated by the report of the gun to hear the spell go off, but the subsequent destruction of the magical turret sent dirt and grass flying.

"Wow, that's a powerful spell," the wolf said behind his smoking gun.

"Take out all the ones along the sidewalk Duncan. Can you hit the one on the sidewalk or is it a different kind?" the captain asked.

"It's different. I can't see it from here. It probably is the landmine kind."

"Carr, send in another potato."

"Right away, Captain."

Carr looked like that guy from that old Rambo movie the way he was holding his potato cannon. Brayton wondered how hard they were to make and if Honey would like to shoot one with him.

Brayton's ears were ringing when Duncan finally lowered his gun a couple of minutes later. He lip-read rather than heard Duncan say, "I hit everything I could see within twenty feet of the entry."

"What do you see Albert?" the captain called back to the van.

"Looks clear. The house is lit up brighter than a Christmas tree though."

"Lovely," the captain muttered, then yelled. "Shields and breakers, you're up, and you," she said, turning on Brayton. "We'll probably need that key to get in the house."

"Don't you have your own magic keys?" Grandpa asked.

"We didn't expect to have to break in when we got this assignment."

"Your lack of preparation does not give you the right to endanger my grandson."

"I can open it," Vera said. She'd been so quiet Brayton had forgotten she was there.

"We've got to get there first," Duncan said. "The aunt is replanting the spells." He lifted the gun and fired at the glowing ball that had just exited out a small round hole that had appeared next to a window on the second story.

Vera made a throwing motion that ended with her hand pointed at the hole. A big glob of water came from somewhere and wobbled through the air, past the glow around the house, and filled the hole, where it solidified.

"How many of those charms does she have?" the captain asked Vera.

"Thousands. Lots of different ones. All sorted into bins and ready to use to defend the house, but…"

Another porthole appeared followed by a big bang and a puff of smoke. The back of the van the captain had suggested Brayton and his grandpa sit in exploded.

"The house is also equipped with cannons," Vera noted, "but not the potato kind."

"They're still cannons. I like this house," Duncan said.

"You would," the captain huffed. "Tate, Aretha, conjure us up some protection. Leave a way in."

Another vehicle exploded.

"We can't leave if you destroy all the vehicles," the captain yelled.

The spell-woman popped up in the yard. "Leave then, but my niece stays here."

"Who do you have in there with you?" Vera demanded.

"You'll have to come inside to find out."

"What do you mean she's got someone with her?" the captain asked.

"She can't move things. Someone else is loading the cannons and throwing the spells," Vera replied then asked, "What are you hoping to achieve aunt? No one will attend school here anymore. We're going to have to shut down."

"It doesn't matter. There's enough money for you to live off the interest."

"And do what? Stay in the house all day?"

"Study. Learn. Become the best witch you can be and someday I'll find a husband for you so the family line will continue."

"That's not the life I want. That's not a life anyone would want."

"That's the way I lived and it was a good life."

"You were never alive. You're a spell!"

"You know what I mean."

"No! I will not…"

"Wait," Brayton interrupted. "Come." He made a motion for Vera to follow him to the van where van man still sat.

"Where are you taking her?" the spell-woman demanded.

"Paper," Brayton explained, knowing it didn't explain anything.

"My grandson is suffering the aftereffects of a spell which makes it difficult to talk. He wants to write something down for her," Grandpa said behind him.

"Oh, you're that kid who resisted the extractor," Duncan exclaimed. "Nicely done."

"Thanks."

"Weren't you attacked by a fire witch and lost an eye too?" the potato cannon wolf asked.

"Yes."

"You can't tell."

Brayton nodded.

"Shame, shame on the witch that gave you that eye. She should be quartered and burned," the spell-witch spat.

"Wow, is she always like that?" Duncan asked.

"She hates wolves," Vera said behind Brayton.

Brayton stuck his head inside the van the man kept yelling from. It was not crowded with computers and TV screens like he'd envisioned, but instead had several mirrors and what looked like fabric stretch over square frames. Van man was monitoring one of the fabric squares. It showed an outline of the house, but it was grainy, like it had been drawn with magnetic fragments instead of a marker. The whole screen glowed with magic until Brayton blinked off his magic vision, then it only glowed around the house and in spots around the yard.

"Paper? Pen?" he asked the man inside.

The man flipped up the clear lens on the glasses he was wearing. "Yes, I have some. Wow, that is a nice eye. Beautiful magic."

"Works," Brayton agreed, wondering if the man could tell his eye could see magic too.

"And your bracelet, may I?"

He lifted Brayton's arm to thoroughly inspect the hairband Honey had given him. "Nicely done. Quality work."

He glanced where the key hung under Brayton's shirt next. Brayton covered it up. "No."

It didn't phase the guy. He peered past Brayton to Vera. "The earrings and the necklace are a matching set, right?"

"Yes."

"Do they record or just send the information back to whoever is monitoring them?"

Vera grabbed at the pendant under her shirt. "They're for protection."

"Only if the person listening comes to your rescue," van man informed her.

"Ooo, that woman." Vera reached up and jerked an earring off her ear.

Brayton expected blood, but there was nothing but a little circle.

"Clip-on," Vera explained at his curious look while she jerked the second one off before reaching back to unhook her necklace. "Aunt wouldn't allow me to pierce my ears, but it was just fine to let my mother rot in a wall."

"Reflexive protection," van man said, nodding to himself, "Nice."

"What do you see?" Vera asked.

"Your jewelry was trying to influence you to do something, probably not take it off. That bracelet you're wearing prevented it."

She held out her hand with the necklace and earrings to the van man. "Do you have somewhere I can stash these so my aunt can't use them to spy on me anymore?"

Van man held up a pen-shaped object. "I can destroy the spells."

"Do it."

"Vera Amelie Lambert," her aunt's voiced boomed much louder than should be possible. "Those are priceless family heirlooms. Don't you dare destroy those spells."

Van man raised an eyebrow at Vera. She nodded decisively and lifted her hand toward his pen.

"Wait," Brayton said. "Anger not."

He pulled an empty, used manila envelope out of the mishmash of objects stuffed into a netted pocket beside the door and offered it to Vera. She dumped the jewelry inside then tossed the closed envelope out the door.

"Good riddance. They didn't go with anything anyway. What did you want to tell me, Brayton, right?"

"Yes." He grabbed a pen from the cup clamped onto the small table near the door and a scrap of paper from the pocket net and wrote, "*You are the only person who can safely get inside. Make a deal with her to ensure you stay safe. Take something to shut her down with you.*"

Vera took the pen from him and wrote, "*She'll detect*

229

anything magical I take with me."

Brayton held his ring up in front of the van man's face. "Magical?"

"May..be? It's very faint if it is."

He slipped it off and set it on the paper and wrote. "*Spell killer. Just touch. Be careful. It's a loaner.*"

Vera picked it up and slipped it in her pocket. "She'd notice," she tapped where it would be on her finger if she wore it.

"Your aunt can travel anywhere in the house and grounds, right?" van man asked.

"Yes."

"But you know where her core is?" he asked in a quieter voice.

"She hangs around the most near the library and the office."

"Can you touch her core?"

"Touch it?"

"Yes," Van man nodded. "A spell like that requires a lot of stored power and complicated spellwork, generally written. It might a book with an energy crystal or crystals on the cover, or a small chest with crystals, or maybe just a large crystal like the one your aunt claimed she trapped the girl in. It would be strong enough you could feel the power."

Vera shook her head. "We don't have anything like that, not in the library."

"Somewhere else?"

Vera frowned and nibbled on her lip, then took the pen from Brayton and wrote, "*The bunker. She probably won't let me close though, not after today. She might have even lowered the bomb door.*"

"Bomb door?" Brayton lipped.

Vera nodded, then wrote. "*The whole room is a magically reinforced bunker. If there's ever a tornado or a bomb, that's the safest place anyone could be.*"

"I'm guessing it holds your family's most precious artifacts," van man said.

"Yeah," Vera sighed. "Too bad there's no family to enjoy them."

"Still you," Brayton said, running his finger over the edge of one of the coins Honey had given him in his pocket. He didn't want to put Honey into any more danger, but if there was a chance she could get another curse tablet, she'd want to take it. If Vera went in there and couldn't shut down the spell, Honey would probably never get the tablet, not easily. Plus, she'd want to help Vera.

He pulled out the smaller of the two coins and put the penny Honey had given him face up on the paper to see if the van man could detect the magic and took the pen from Vera. "*Lucky penny. Put face up in front of the bunker door or, if you can't get there, in the middle of the closest floor.*"

She picked it up and inspected it. "What does it do?"

"Nothing. Lucky," he said, then wrote, "*Trust me. Whatever you do though, don't drop it into anything small like a drain. That would be bad. It needs space.*"

Van man's eyes got big. "Oh, is that…" he grabbed the pen from Brayton and wrote, "*One of those iron-man transformation spells where the penny turns into a little magical superhero?*"

"Sort of." That existed?

"*Wow. I can barely detect anything magical about it at all,*" van man wrote.

231

Brayton took the pen from him and wrote, "*Vera, the penny is your back-up. How long should I give you before I activate the spell?*"

"I don't know. Aunt might trap me in a spell as punishment."

"*When you make your deal, keeping the hairband must be part of it. It will protect you.*"

"She won't allow it."

"*Then no deal. No punishment either, or curses. She has to agree not to harm you or cause your death either directly or by neglect.*"

"Better be very specific about how you word things," van man said.

"I'm aware. I've been dealing with her my whole life." She took the pen from Brayton and wrote, "*Give me an hour. Send help if nothing happens after that.*"

He nodded and wrote, "*Okay, but put the coin down heads up at your first opportunity. You don't want it in your pocket when it goes off. Trust me.*"

HONEY – STILL MORNING – CANADA

"Honey?"

Honey set the stack of books she was carrying on the librarian's cart. *"Yes. Is everything okay? I saw on the news that you went to Texas and were in front of the school trying to turn off Philomena."*

"Far so. See. Vera Lambert. Inside go?"

"Yeah."

"Ring has my. Needs maybe help she. Penny her gave."

"You trust her?"

"Ish. Alone. Sad. Near curse be may core."

"The curse may be stored near the core? What core?"

"Philomena. Bunker in. Protected very."

"Did you need something?" the young librarian asked.

Honey shook her head and moved away from the cart she'd been hovering over during her silent conversation with Brayton.

"Thanks for your help collecting the books. It's nice to see people interested in reading, but the cleanup," the librarian finished with a sigh and a long look over the tables still covered with books.

Honey gave her a single nod and moved to collect the books from the next table. *"Any chance it's a trap?"* she asked.

"Possible. Coming you doesn't know are. Thinks Iron Man penny."

"Iron Man penny?"

"Into turns."

"Really? You told her it turned into Iron Man and she believed you?"

"Me not. Another. Witch."

"What's the plan?"

"Signal on appear you. Destroy. Philomena."

"You're going to give me a signal to pop into a possibly hostile witch's house with a very hostile spell that wants me dead?"

"Yes. No. Honey…"

She grinned at his plaintive whining. *"I'm teasing. Sounds like fun."*

"Fun not. Dangerous. Fault my."

"Brayton. Stop. I can do this. I'm made for this."

"Know I. Worried."

"I know."

"Love you."

Did he? Her stomach did a little flip. *"I know."*

Honey scooped up the large pile of books she'd stacked while she was communicating with Brayton and spun around, right into something that hadn't been there before. The books flew out of her arms and scattered all over the table and the floor.

"Oh, sorry," the guy who'd snuck up on her said.

Honey glanced up at him and then quickly down when she realized it was the same guy she'd argued with earlier. Had he done that on purpose? Had he recognized her somehow? How though? She was wearing completely different clothes. She was now dressed as a guy in Jay's clothes, all rolled up to fit her, with a different beanie and no glasses or wig. Keeping her head down, she slunk to the book on the floor farthest around the table before squatting below the level of the table to begin cleaning up the mess.

"Let me help," the guy said, coming around the table and squatting right next to her.

She gathered the few books she'd already collected to her chest and popped up and away from him. Leaving him to clean up the rest of them, she dumped the books she was holding onto the cart and went to a different table.

None of the books on the new table had promising titles either. She stacked them all up, shot a quick glance to where the sneaky guy had last been to make sure he was still there, then hauled the load to the cart.

"Wow, you're strong," the librarian noted.

"Thanks," Honey said in a deep voice.

"Hey," the librarian said in a quieter tone, "did something happen between you and that guy? He keeps glaring at you."

"No."

"I could ask him to leave."

"No. I have to go soon. Do you have a book on water retrieval spells or artifacts?"

"For sure! I'll show you. What are you trying to retrieve?"

"Treasure," Honey made up.

"I know just the books." The girl sashayed over to a section painted in blue and waved her hand at a series of books with water and gold coins on the binders. "The author goes all over the world looking for lost treasure. He has a YouTube channel too."

"Thanks."

"Sure," she said perkily, then looked back at the artifact section and sighed. "I better get back to sorting."

Honey pulled out the first book knowing it probably wasn't going to be helpful, but hoping the introduction came with a description of techniques. The introduction consisted of the guy's name and what he was searching for, but his style was arresting, and before she knew it, she was ten pages in.

A hand clamped down on the back of her neck. She automatically twisted and used her shoulder and elbow to knock the hand away while moving to get her own grip on the attacker's throat. It was the same guy, but with his eyes rolled back into his head. Great, a diviner. He could probably see right through her costume.

"Go now," he whispered.

"Go where?"

"Is everything all right here?" the older librarian, the one who knew Honey from before, asked a few tables away.

"Yeah. He's having a vision I think," Honey said in her deepest voice and shifted her hand to hold his shoulder instead of his throat.

"Best sit him down then," the kind woman said, bustling over.

The guy looked at Honey, but with his eyes full white. "No. Go now. Girl in danger. Take me."

"Why?" Honey asked.

"Needs me."

Could he be fooling her? Was it possible to make eyes roll back like that without magic? Could he possibly be working with Philomena? She didn't see how. Honey touched the bookshelf with her wrist just in case she'd need to come back.

"What's he talking about?" the librarian asked.

236

"Rescue mission. I gotta go." To the guy she said, "Hold your breath," although she doubted it mattered since he was still in the midst of his vision.

37

HONEY - 11:30 AM - TEXAS

Honey landed with her cheek against a cold cement floor and the irritating guy laying over her like an extremely heavy mannequin. Above them, the air was hazy with magic. She pulled in a layer of air to protect her nose, then carefully scooted out from under the guy who appeared to still be lost in a vision.

"Stop it Aunt!"

A bolt like lightning, but more magical, shot out from a sturdy iron cage the size of a pineapple on top of a chunky pedestal toward a girl standing near a shelf full of glowing magical objects. The girl dodged but she wasn't fast enough. Instead of zapping her though, the lightning turned into a dimmer glow that dissipated a few inches from the surface of her skin.

"Take off the shield Vera," Philomena's voice boomed much louder than a human could make without speakers.

"I will not let you erase my memories!"

Philomena was nowhere to be seen but based on the power level of whatever was inside the cage, it was probably important for her spell, which meant the glowing object likely had shields upon shields upon shields. Fun. Honey slipped off two of her hairbands and put them on mannequin boy's wrist then shifted over a few feet so anything directed at her wouldn't hit him. Another bolt shot towards Vera. Again, the hairband shield protected her. It wouldn't last much longer though, Honey was sure. She better get to work.

Conjuring up the strongest magical shield she could, she bent it into a razor-sharp point, then thrust it forward, hard. It stabbed through the onion-like layers that surrounded the cage like a freshly sharpened knife. She made the shield expand and push layers open until she had a clear view of the intricate cage underneath.

Ignoring the screaming and yelling in several different pitches that Philomena was trying to distract her with, and the bolts of magic pounding her secondary shield, Honey stalked forward. The iron was cursed with a blood curse by the smell. She wondered who had given their life for it. The magic of it flowed and pulsed through the holes like twisting snakes. She poked her finger with a claw and flicked her blood at it to get its attention.

The magic snake slithered out and around the cage and began to grow both longer and wider, all the while slithering over itself.

"What are you protecting?" Honey asked the snake's head.

"My creation, the spell who protects this house. You are cursed to add your blood to its protection," a woman's voice screamed. It sounded like Philomena's but scratchier. Was she speaking to the real Philomena's essence now?

"Your spell has killed off all your family members except one and was trying to hurt her when I got here. Let me disable it and perhaps you can transfer your curse to something else, perhaps to protect the house from those who mean the family harm."

"You lie."

"Ask her. She's right there." Honey nodded to Vera who was watching from the other side of the room pressed up against the wall like someone had plastered her there.

"Lie. Lie. Lie. My spell protects. She can't kill."

"She did though. Indirectly. She trapped people in a picture without food."

"Lie. Lie. Lie."

"Oh, for Pete's sake," Honey grumbled. "The curse is as bad as the spell."

The snake was huge now, more than big enough to swallow her if it wanted. What was it waiting for?

"Vera, can you see the snake?"

"What snake?"

"That's good. Can you drag that guy that came with me toward the door."

"I can walk," a voice said behind her.

"Can you see the snake?" Honey asked out of curiosity.

"Y-yes."

"Interesting."

She didn't dare take her eyes off the snake, but she wasn't comfortable with Mr. Sneaky behind her, nor did she want to freeze him and leave him unable to move with the snake present.

"Are you okay?" She asked to keep the conversation going and so she could tell where he was.

"Yeah. You need to destroy that thing."

"I'm aware."

"Or it will kill us all."

"Lovely. Any idea how to do that?"

The snake lunged. She jumped high and to the side.

"No," the guy said, now to her left and farther back.

Good. The snake would keep him away.

"Did you see it kill us or are you guessing?"

"Guessing mostly."

If that hadn't been a future or past vision that meant he was probably a truth diviner.

"You know who I am?"

"Yes?"

"That's what you saw?"

"Yes. You are my cousin."

If he was trying to distract her from the snake, he failed. She dove and rolled out of the way of the lunging snake's fangs.

"Cousin? I didn't think my mom had any siblings," she said while popping to her feet.

"Third cousin, once removed."

"Is Vera a cousin too? You said she needed you."

"No."

"Give her one of those hair bands I put on your wrist. Hers is about depleted I think."

Honey jumped straight up when the snake lunged again and this time landed on the snake's back. To her surprise, she didn't go through it. This was one strong curse.

The snake flung her toward the low ceiling where there was nothing to grab onto but an ancient hanging light bulb that looked like it had been installed when electricity was first invented. She did the only thing she could safely do to avoid decorating the ceiling with her face. She threw herself into the nether and back to the penny on the floor.

In the short few seconds she was gone, the snake had

focused on her self-proclaimed cousin and backed him against a door. She leaped to her feet and ran toward him, forging a huge Frisbee-shaped shield with a razor-like edge at the same time. She threw it just as the snake reared back. She thought at first that she might have missed, but instead of lunging toward her cousin, the snake's head did a slow slide backwards, then the whole body collapsed and melted into the floor.

She felt something behind her and dove to the side before she looked to see what it was. Another snake, another head, another mouth full of fangs. This one was smaller but quicker. She barely made it to her feet before it lunged again. She leapt and flung another frisbee-shield beneath her at its retreating head.

A third snake was waiting for her when she turned around. Well, waiting wasn't quite correct. It was already lunging. Luckily, it was only the size of a large cobra. She grabbed it by the neck and lobbed the head off with the flick of a shield which she extended around herself before the animal had finished dissolving. More snakes appeared, small ones, all trying to break through her shield. Why though? What was the point? Were they trying to distract her or was a bite how the curse chose its victim? Since the little snakes couldn't get through her shield, she lifted her head to take stock of the situation.

"You two okay?"

"Yeah," Vera called out from the direction of the door. "We're trying to figure out how to get out of here."

"Any snakes over there, cous?"

"No. How long does it usually take you to break a curse?"

"Depends on the curse. It can be seconds to days."

"Sooner would be better."

"No kidding."

Honey closed her eyes and focused on her sense of smell. Metal, blood, cement, power: all things she'd expect from what she could see, but she also smelled the sheets that she associated with illusions and fresh water that reminded her of a little creek in the woods where they had WOLF classes. On top of all that was the almost overwhelming smell of cotton candy and…formaldehyde? The water smell, which she associated with Vera, wasn't coming from the direction of the door, but from the center of the room where the formaldehyde smell originated. She focused through the mist which she now recognized for what it was, a way to hide all the lines of power circling the room and the ones going right to the Vera she could see. The lines all flowed across the floor, up the stone pillar, and to cage on top of it, but was that truly the source of the magic or was it an illusion too?

She formed another sharp-edged Frisbee shield, but this time used it to slice through the lines of power at the base of the stone.

"What are you doing?" Vera asked in alarm.

"Testing an idea."

She sent the second slice between the metal cage and the top of the pillar, willing it to go around any bolts holding it on, but to slice through any magic.

"Nooo…"

"Where did she go?" her cousin, if that's what he was, asked.

"That wasn't Vera. Did you give her the hair band?"

"She wouldn't take it."

"That's because the spell has already captured her."

243

Keeping her shield up, although the small snakes had all disappeared with Vera, Honey approached the pillar again. Not really wanting to touch the cage, she kicked the pillar toe first to see if was as solid as it looked. To her surprise, it shifted easily. Her second kick was one she'd used to break boards and to kick a certain irritating alpha-to-be across the cafeteria. It worked pretty much the same on the pillar, which shot out from under the cage and crashed into the far wall.

"How is that hanging there?" her cousin asked from much closer than he'd been before. She was seriously going to have to put a bell on him.

"Good question."

She walked around the cage looking for the answer twice before she thought to feel above it for ropes or whatever was holding it up. It wasn't rope. To her surprise, she met solid resistance starting at the cage and going up.

"No way."

"What?" her cousin asked, again right behind her, although she knew he was there this time.

"It's a stair, but it's painted to match the background so well it's basically invisible. The cage isn't a cage at all. It's part of the stairs, which means those spells I destroyed were meant to keep me from going up the stairs, not prevent me from touching the cage."

She followed the invisible metal down with her hand until it came to a stop three feet above the floor, the same height the pillar had been.

"I bet the pillar provides support for the stair when it is in the up position like it is now." She pulled down. It had been months since she'd climbed or did pull-ups, but the spiral stairs lowered easily. The steps were more visible now that they no longer matched their background. As she had suspected, the glowing lines of Philomena's spell went up the center of the pole instead of stopping at the cage.

"I'm going up. If you follow me, stay back at least four steps. I'll need room."

"Sure," he said, right in her ear.

She ran up the stairs with a strong shield ready in front of her, but all she encountered was a door. She ripped through the spells on the door with the sharp edge of her shield and sent it to the nether. The wards behind the door were nearly blinding with strength, but with effort, she cut through them too. Immediately, a bolt of magic shot out from the center of the room. Honey dove inside, keeping her shield up between her and the glow from the center of the room.

"Who is that?" her shadow asked, peering around the door toward the center of the room.

"Are you trying to get zapped?" Honey snapped.

"She's after you, not me."

"That," Honey said indicating the chair where a shriveled old lady with a helmet of glowing lines sat, "is the real Philomena."

"Where's Vera?"

"I don't know, but she's here."

"You die here, hybrid," the room screamed at her, and a powerful something zapped her from behind.

Over the stench of candy and preservative Honey smelled at least one of her hair bands burning up in her defense. The lightning shouldn't have gotten through. She was being sloppy. She rolled and charged. Another big snake with a mouth large enough to swallow a grizzly's head sprouted out of the floor in front of her. She flung her shield at it, chopping off its head as she spun around it and threw another shield directly at the old woman's face. As soon as it hit her target, she made it bend around the old woman's face, forming a solid globe around the head so that the shield blocked any signal from the woman's head to the spell lines running all through the house. Except for the globe that was the woman's head, the room went dark.

"Vera, where are you? Can you hear me?"

Something moved on her left. Honey spun to see what it was and barely got her arm up in time to prevent an ax from cleaving her head in two.

"Die! Why won't you die? This is all your fault."

Honey jerked the ax out of Vera's hands. "What's my fault? Your crazy aunt hooking herself up to magic well before I was born, I might add, and killing off her family?"

"She didn't kill them!"

"Who did then?"

"They died of natural c-causes."

"She's been brain-washed," Honey's creepy cousin said from the dark, again way closer than he should have been.

Honey froze Vera's body so she wouldn't attack again and glared in the direction of her cousin. "Stop sneaking up on me and find a light switch, if there is one, or a candle. I'm not picky."

"Show me what you are, what you truly are," he demanded.

"You're a diviner. You know what I am." She pulled up another shield, not that it would do much good against anything solid, if that's how he was planning to attack her.

"I don't see you like I see other people. I see a glow, like the moon, and infinite darkness. Are you the light in the darkness or the darkness swallowing the light?"

She popped into wolf form more to see her surroundings better than to appease him. He was right where she'd guessed he was. The rest of the room looked quiet and a bit spooky with a glowing head attached to a dark body in the middle of the room. She didn't see a light switch, but she did spot a candle. With all her recent campfire-lighting practice, it only took a few seconds to light the candle. She glanced at him one more time, shook out her glowing fur, because why not, and popped back into her human form.

"Satisfied?"

"Monster!" Vera cried.

"Can you fix her?" her cousin asked.

Somewhere in the house there was a crash.

"What's going on Vera?" Honey asked.

"They are coming for you."

"Get us out of here," her cousin said, stepping closer and offering Honey his hand. "Before they find you."

"We have time. Pull up the stairs. I need the curse tablet. Vera, where's the tablet?"

"Like I would tell you, monster!"

Honey forced herself to be calm. "Vera, what's the last thing you remember?"

"You, breaking into our house."

"I've never broken in. Your aunt invited me in, but that was months ago. When did I break in?"

"An hour ago. You locked me in a closet. You killed my mother and father and grandmother."

"Didn't your grandmother die before you were born?"

247

"My mother and father then," she claimed after the smallest of pauses.

"I wasn't born yet when your father disappeared."

"My mother then," she sniffed.

"I would have been seven."

"You started young."

The room brightened. Honey glanced over her shoulder to where her cousin was lighting more candles. "What's your name anyway, cous?"

"Michael."

"You're not Michael! Michael had red hair. He disappeared. He said he loved me then he disappeared," Vera said sadly.

"I'm not that Michael, I'm a different Michael," her cousin said, crossing the room to grab Vera's hand. Not only was he able to move it – Vera must be thawing out – but he lifted it to his lips and kissed her fingers. "But I won't leave you unless you want me to."

Honey forced her eyebrows down. "Do you know each other?"

"We do now," Michael said, still holding Vera's hand.

Somewhere below, she heard another bang. That one sounded more like a door slamming open. Right, a door. She walked over to the empty doorway and put the one she'd removed back. It was backwards but would do to keep the searchers from seeing the light.

Honey pretended she didn't hear Vera's whispered, "We have to trap her, she's evil." Instead, she walked to the other side of the room and started inspecting the dusty shelves. Most of the items were broken or disassembled, and only a few held magic.

"This must have been your aunt's workshop," she

248

commented.

"The tablet isn't here," Vera proclaimed.

"Did you know your aunt had used her own brain to program the spell that looked like her?" Honey asked, turning abruptly just in case one or both of them were sneaking up on her. They weren't.

"No," Vera said, glancing, then looking away from the shriveled body.

Michael pulled Vera to his chest so she could hide her head. Vera leaned into him. Odd.

"Do witches have fated mates?" Honey wondered out loud.

"I'm a diviner," Michael said.

"And..."

Michael shook his head and put his finger over his lips.

"Tell her what happened. Maybe she'll believe you."

"I can do better than that." He looked tenderly down at Vera. "Can I share my memories with you?"

Vera looked up at him with such a look of trust, Honey wanted to shake her. No woman should look at a man like that five minutes after meeting him.

"Close your eyes," he said softly, then pushed his fingers into Vera's hair and placed his thumbs on her forehead.

"Stop. Just stop." They both looked at her in surprise. "Vera, you just met this guy! I just met this guy, and you're trusting him with your brain?"

"I'm a diviner, I can't really do much but share things. I'm just going to show her what I saw on TV," Michael said.

"You could read her mind."

"I don't have any big secrets," Vera said defiantly.

249

"Oh yeah? Where's the curse tablet?"

"In the bunker," she sniffed, "but you can't touch it without me. You have to have Lambert blood to get through the protections."

"Have you ever touched it?" Honey asked curiously.

"No. Why would I?"

"Just curious. Carry on I suppose. It's your brain."

"You won't hurt me will you?" Vera asked Michael, blinking her big blue eyes up at him.

"Never," he declared.

Honey couldn't smell a lie, but then she couldn't smell much over the candy and formaldehyde smell that was quickly turning into something less pleasant. She couldn't hear anything in the room downstairs either. There was a good chance the Enforcers hadn't found it yet. Dare she try and retrieve the tablet?

Yes, yes she dared.

"You guys take your time. I'll be back, maybe," she said, then sent herself to the nether again.

HONEY – TEXAS BUNKER, DOWNSTAIRS

Honey cautiously lifted her face off the floor. People were yelling and talking somewhere in the house, but the bunker was quiet and dark except for the faint glow from a few magical lanterns. How well-hidden was the bunker door? With the spell-woman down, she might only have a few seconds to locate the curse out of the myriad of powerful spells she could smell all around her.

She closed her eyes and, ignoring her nose, tried to feel for the curse while slowly turning. There, maybe? She stepped closer to the shelves lining the back wall. There was definitely something there amid the boxes and boxes of jewelry. No, not in the boxes, higher up.

"You've got to be kidding me."

The ugly necklace she'd been accused of stealing last spring hung prominently on the wall like a gaudy, misplaced sun. Several layers of spells, deadly ones, were woven over it, some of them already aware of her presence.

She lifted her hand and let the guard-dog smell take a sniff. It growled, but as soon as she tickled him under the chin, it was all eager beagle. It was cute too. Was it possible to adopt a guardian spell?

"You're probably all lonely down here, aren't you?"

The spell gave a silent bark and pressed himself into her hand.

"You can come with me if you want."

It whined and looked back at the monstrosity of a necklace.

"I could take it with me."

The spell growled, but it was more of a *'you know better than that'* than a *'I'm going to bite your face off'* kind of growl.

"I don't actually want the necklace. I want the curse tablet that's probably stuck to the back. Can I see if it's there?"

The spell growled again. She made scratching motions behind its transparent ears, earning her another whine and big-eyed look between her and the necklace.

"You are so cute. Seriously, I am the good guy, not that your owners are bad, but if I can destroy the curse, it will be good for everyone. Can I just look?"

If dogs chewed their lips, her new friend would be doing it. It looked back at the necklace, then at her, then back and forth several more times.

"I promise, I won't take the necklace, just the curse tablet." She stuck out her hand. "Here, climb on. You can sit on my shoulder and bite me if I try to trick you."

The dog shrank to the size of a weasel and ran up her arm to settle on her shoulder. She scratched where she imagined its head was. "You would be a good travel companion. Okay, let's see if I can get through the rest of the spells."

Either she was getting better, or the spells were weak. All she had to do was slice at them with another sharp-edged shield and they fell away.

Without the spells, the magical glow of the necklace and its chain was more noticeable. Honey put her nose as close as she dared to the chain and took a sniff with her new friend growling softly in her ear.

"Smells like a trap. What, are you forced to wear this thing after you touch it? That's awful. What does the pendant part do?" she sniffed at the magically bright sun. "Smells like power and pain and fire." She stepped back and scratched her new friend's head. "Are you protecting the artifact or are you protecting people from touching it, because that thing would probably kill someone."

Her new friend chomped down on her finger. Even though the spell didn't have real teeth, she felt the bite. Before she could chastise it, the dark room disappeared and was replaced by trees and sunshine filtering through a canopy of summer leaves onto a small, grassy clearing by a tiny creek. Everything smelled real, down to the mud in the creek and warm grass, but mostly it smelled of magic. Before she could decide what kind of magic it was, a woman in a long dress and long sleeves that reminded Honey strongly of Guinevere in a movie she'd seen once, walked gracefully through the tree trunks.

"Hail sister."

She sounded like Guinevere too.

"Hail to you," Honey replied politely. "Who are you and where am I?"

"I am Mother Lambert, and whom might thou be?"

That was a tricky question. She was pretty sure though that her name would make no difference to this woman.

"Honey."

"Sweet Honey for a sweet wench, I'm sure. Thou are not of my blood."

"No."

"How didst thou come to hast possession of mine talisman?"

"I am not in possession of it. You are in possession of me."

The woman laughed. "So I am. Art thou surprised? O' course thou are." She paused and her features readjusted into a stern glare. "Why were thou trying to steal mine talisman?"

"I was not trying to steal it. I was trying to find the curse tablet and I felt it near the talisman."

"Thou can feel it?"

"Yes."

"What doth thou desire with it?"

"To break it."

"That would not be wise. 'Tis the only way to prevent the Black Death."

"The curse doesn't prevent the black death. The plague wasn't caused by magic."

"What was the cause then?"

"It was just a horrible disease. We have ways to cure it now."

"It's still around?" the woman snapped.

Honey was pretty certain the Mother Lambert speaking to her was the same woman she'd seen in the vision in the museum. How could she explain bacteria to a spell made in the 1300's?

"Maybe. It's not clear. It is definitely not spreading the way it did in your time."

"Then the curse worked."

"No. Outbreaks continued to occur until the 1800s," Honey said, quoting the Wiki article she'd read.

"What century is it now?"

"The twenty-first."

"What of mine line, are there any left?"

"One, that I know of."

"And where is she?"

"Upstairs."

"Retrieve her."

Abruptly, Honey landed on her rear in the dark again. The bunker was quiet, but somewhere outside it she could hear muffled voices talking, not yelling. How well-hidden was the door?

"I think, it would be best if I took you to her," she said softly, in case the woman could hear her.

Not wanting to mess with whatever spell was on the talisman, Honey pulled a pair of sunglasses from the nether, carefully lifted the chain off its hook with the leg, then sent herself and it to the nether and back into the upstairs room just in time to witness Vera haul back and slap Michael. Honey immediately froze his body so he couldn't retaliate.

"What did he do?"

"He got inside my head, then he kissed me."

"There's probably a law against that. If not, there should be," Honey mused.

"That's not what happened!" Michael protested.

"What happened then?" Honey asked.

"I showed her what I saw, then I realized she found me attractive. I thought she wanted me to kiss her."

"News flash, you can't use your powers to read a woman's mind. That's cheating," Honey informed him.

"All's fair in love..."

"...and war," Vera said, slapping him on the other cheek, although not as hard.

"Anyway," Honey said, lifting the talisman, "your ancestor wants to speak to you. I'm not sure how you're…" she broke off as the guardian spell jumped off the chain and ran toward Vera.

"My ancestor?"

"Vera! Watch out!" Michael warned.

"Yes. I think it's Maria Lambert but you can ask her," Honey finished right before the guardian bit Vera on the ankle and she disappeared.

"Where did she go? What have you done with her?" Michael demanded.

"I didn't do anything. What's up between you and Vera? Why are you coming on to her so strong?" Honey automatically scratched behind the guardian's ears when he came back to her and leaned against her leg.

"I dream about her, okay."

Honey carefully set the necklace on the counter, sent her sunglasses back to the nether, then squatted to give the guardian a good rub.

"Recently?"

"Since I was five. What are you doing?"

"Petting the guardian spell. He likes having his ears rubbed."

"And you would know just where to rub because you're basically part dog."

"Exactly. If you can see spells then you know you don't want to touch that necklace," she warned when he started to thaw and lean toward it, "it's likely a very painful way to die."

"But Vera's in there."

"You can feel her?"

He nodded without taking his eyes off the talisman.

"I think it's safe. The woman in there just talked to me and then kicked me out."

256

The guardian straightened and made a little grunt that she interpreted as 'be right back', then charged at Michael.

"What's he doing? Did you sic him on me?!"

Before she could answer him, the guardian bit him and he disappeared too.

She'd been in a lot of scary situations but being alone in a dark room with a shriveled body and a glowing head was one of the creepiest.

"Guess I should put the door back the right way," she told the guardian.

He sat down at her feet as if to say, *'I'll wait right here.'*

She blew out all the candles but one, then did exactly as she'd said. The bunker below was still dark and quiet. She was strongly tempted to stay on the other side of the door out on the landing, but she didn't trust Philomena not to figure out a way past her shield. With a sigh, she popped back into the room. The guardian greeted her like a long-lost friend.

"Brayton, are you there?" Honey sent after several long minutes had passed.

"Yes."

"Are you still at Vera's house?"

"Yes. Watching."

"I'm inside."

"Spell you down brought?" he asked after a pause.

"Yes, basically. Philomena was powering the spell with her own brain. I'm in the hidden room with her body now. It's creepy."

"Coming they."

"I know. I can hear them. It might take them a while to find this place though."

"Find curse?"

257

"Umm, maybe. There's another spell-woman, but she's in that ugly necklace they tried to frame me for stealing. I think it's Marie Lambert. Vera is talking to her now. The necklace has a very friendly guardian spell, but I would not recommend touching the necklace itself. I think the curse tablet is in the necklace too."

"In?"

"Yeah. I'm not sure how it works, but the necklace can suck in a person whole. There are trees and a creek in there, and sunshine, and air. I could feel the tablet more strongly when I was in the necklace."

The guardian she was still petting tilted his head like he was listening to something, then showed his teeth, not in a growl though. It was more like *'I'm going to bite you again, be ready'*.

"Looks like I've been invited inside again. Talk to you later."

"Honey…"

She didn't hear the rest of what Brayton said due to the teeth clamped on her finger.

"Discover me thy wolf," Madame Lambert said as soon as Honey materialized in front of her.

"Excuse me?"

"She wants to see your wolf, I think," Michael said on her right. Vera stood beside him looking pale and wan.

"Are you okay Vera?"

"Yes," Vera replied, dropping her head to look down at her feet.

It was the saddest yes Honey had ever heard. Honey ached to comfort her, but she wasn't sure what to say, so she focused on Michael instead. "Why does she want to see my wolf?"

"I think she wants to see," he tapped his forehead.

"You told her about that?"

"I told her everything."

"Everything? Even about what I've been blamed for?"

"Yes."

Honey didn't bother suppressing her sigh.

"I wot thou are not cursed," the medieval woman said. "The forbidden would not be able to stand ere me as thou are. Thou are something else. Something Methought was only a myth."

"And what is that?"

"Show me your wolf and I will tell you."

Honey made sure her shield was strong, then popped into wolf form. She stayed that way for a few moments, then transformed back.

Madame Lambert smiled and nodded, then recited,

"Beautiful, rare be the Celestial Luna.
Chosen by one who's life is at end.
Marked by the moon, she glows 'i the darkness.
Marked by the stars, she shines 'i the sun.
No knave exists, her will can resist.
Nay alpha her equal, alone she stands.
Yet powerful be, the one whom can claim her.
Not perforce yet by love,
Her heart must he win."

"You think I am a Celestial Luna?"

"Doth thou not hast stars across thou brow and fur so white it glows?"

"I guess."

"And where is the alpha whom chose thou?"

"He is…gone."

"Dead?" the woman asked bluntly.

"Yes." Honey blinked to clear her eyes of tears, but didn't take her eyes off the woman, even though she sensed Michael shift beside her.

Madame Lambert nodded. "It is as I hast surmised. I hast a proposition for thou."

"And what is that?"

"I shall grant thou our part of the curse if thou join mine descendant's hand with that of thy relative and consent to join to their aid 'i times of necessity."

"You want me to help them if they ever need it," Honey translated, "and, what do you mean by join their hands?"

"Is that not how thou say marry these days?"

"No, that's right, but I'm not sure what you want of me. I have no problem with them getting married, but I have no say in it either."

Madame Lambert smiled in the way older people did when a younger person showed how clueless they were. "I would just as I quoth. Thou shall to join their hands, both literally and magically."

"Me?!"

Madame Lambert gave a solemn nod. "Thou are a Celestial Luna, above e'en the alphas, and the direct issue of a powerful witch clan. A binding by one so graced shall be blessed."

Honey shook her head. "Now-a-days, people are married in the church or by a Justice of the Peace."

"And by the heads of their covens or families," Michael threw in. "And I think alphas are involved in wolf weddings."

"Really?" Honey asked him.

"Aunt Philomena presided over my mother and grandmother's weddings," Vera said to her feet, "although we know how that turned out."

"Do they want to get married?" Honey asked, glancing at Vera and Michael to see their reactions. "They just met."

"It matters not. Mine line needs continue. Vera is of age and the wizard hath agreed. They shall marry and hast many children."

Vera flinched and her head sank even lower. First her aunt and now her super-great grandmother were bossing her around. It wasn't fair. The poor girl should be able to make her own choices.

"They call the males witches now too," Honey informed Madame Lambert, "and it does matter. Vera has had a horrible day and is mourning her family. I doubt she is in the right mind to make decisions that will affect the rest of her life and we only met Michael today. What if he turns out to be an awful person? What if he harms her?"

"Doth thou desire the tablet or not?"

"I do. May I see it before I make a decision?"

"Thou canst not leave mine presence ere I shall allow it," the spell warned her.

"I assumed as much," Honey informed her, "but I'm not sure how this spell world of yours works or how I can detect the tablet outside the necklace even though you say it is inside."

"Thou used a seeking spell?"

"Yes."

"Thou hast located other parts of the curse?"

"Yes."

Madame Lambert nodded. "That is good. I hast aye

suspected we were misled about the cause of the plague, yet we were desperate. The tablet is the blueish boulder near yon creek."

"It's a boulder?" Honey asked.

Madame Lambert gave a single nod. "Mine gift was transmutation."

Honey walked over to the smaller boulder and squatted beside it where she could still face everyone, then held her hand over the top of the stone. It did feel like the curse. "If I destroy it in this form, will it still destroy the curse?"

"The magic and the words are still intact, just 'i a divers form. Should thee crush the stone, they shall be broken. All five pieces must be destroyed together else thou shall unleash a ranker curse."

"What's a ranker curse?" Honey asked.

"More horrible than the first," Madame Lambert explained.

"How could it get worse?"

"Never-ending torture in limbo."

"Limbo?"

"Every young witch should'st wot of limbo. Doth they teach it not these days?"

"I think she means the never," Vera said. "Some people call it the nothing. It's where things go when they vanish."

"You mean the nether?"

"That's another term for it."

"Can people live in the nether?"

"I don't think so. Maybe that's the curse. You keep dying then coming back alive – never ending torture."

Magic couldn't bring a person to life whose soul had

moved on, could it? She'd have to look it up later. She turned her attention back to the spell-woman. "One of my ancestors already destroyed one of the tablets and a tree destroyed another."

"Art thou positive 'twere destroyed?"

"That's what they said." What if her ancestor was wrong? What if they only thought it had been destroyed? Come to think of it, why did the seeking spell not detect the pieces? It had detected the ones under the tree. "Are you sure there's a ranker curse?" Honey asked, tapping the rock with the knuckle of her middle finger to casually attach an anchor. "I can't detect one."

"Enough! Decide."

Honey stood and walked over to Vera and Michael so that she was face-to-face with them.

"Vera," Honey offered her hand to the girl. After a long hesitation, Vera took it. "Michael," Honey offered her hand to him. He took it almost immediately. "Do you want to get married?"

"I don't know," Vera said, looking at her feet. Michael didn't say anything, but the tender look on his face while he gazed at Vera was answer enough.

"It matters not," the spell-woman said. "They are not leaving until they are joined."

"Vera, look at me," Honey urged. When Vera looked up, Honey mimed holding her breath. When she was sure Vera had the message, she threw herself and them into the nether. In the dark of the nether, she jerked her knuckle to pull the stone to her just before sending herself and her two passengers back to Earth.

BRAYTON – 12 PM – TEXAS

"Whoever built this house knew what they were doing," the man in the van whom someone had finally introduced as Albert, commented while tapping the frame of his screen. "Even with the main protection down, I can't see where that bunker is."

Brayton sent Honey one more message in case she was out of the necklace then snapped back into human form. "Not magic?"

"How do you do that? I've never seen a wolf transform so fast, and with clothes too."

Brayton shrugged. Albert frowned, then turned back to his screen. "It's likely underground, but so far we haven't found a way under the house."

"Albert," Captain LeDoux said just outside the van door, "They've cleared the building. Get in there and find the door."

"Go I?" Brayton asked.

"No," the captain snapped. "We've got enough dead bodies to account for."

"Let them do their job," Grandpa said behind the captain. "We'll find out the details soon enough, especially if she's crammed any wolves in the walls." Grandpa stepped closer and whispered, or used what passed as a whisper for him, in Brayton's ear. "Vera's back."

Grandpa glanced to where they'd left Grandma and

Mr. Felix then gave a little tilt of his head to indicate they should move away from the van and the enforcers crowded around it. Once they were about twenty feet away, he said in a low voice, "She says Honey rescued her and her cousin from the necklace...Honey's cousin, not Vera's."

"Zavier?"

"No. On her Wixx side," Grandpa said slowly, still listening. "Mrs. Wixx knows him. Honey's fine. She retrieved the tablet. Ms. Lambert says she knows a spell to retrieve the last one, but she needs access to her library."

"Long time take," Brayton said, eyeing the people in gloves and medical gear who were only now being allowed to enter the building.

"Yes, but there's no rush. That tablet has been down there a long time."

Two enforcers exited the building with a hand-cuffed female witch between them. "That who?"

"Must be the witch who was helping Philomena."

"VU library?" Brayton suggested.

"I think Mrs. Wixx suggested the same thing." Grandpa looked around. Enforcers were swarming all around them, but none were that close. Grandpa grabbed Brayton's arm just as the ground rippled in front of them. "Time for a quick exit." They stepped forward together into the portal that took them to Mr. Felix, then into the second one that landed them back at the college.

NOTES FROM THE AUTHOR

Wow, that cut off abruptly. Sorry. Not trying to be evil. I wrote the series with no goals as to how many books I was aiming for, then chopped it into publishable pieces. There is one more piece after this. It's already written and nearly ready to be published so if it isn't online yet, it should be shortly. Also, the first chapter of the next book is at the end of this one.

Reader feedback is very much appreciated. Please leave a review if you liked the story and tell your friends and your librarian. (That's me marketing. Impressive, right?)

You may have noticed the 'Clean Fiction' logo at the beginning of the book. I love to read but sometimes, okay often, find myself in the middle of a good story and abruptly I'm in someone's bedroom getting a play-by-play. Sex happens but I don't need to be there. I'm not the only one who feels this way. I discovered whole communities on social media and a magazine devoted to clean reads. To make it easier for like-minded people to find clean books and to encourage other authors to go clean, I thought a logo on said books would be helpful. So, if you are a writer or know one and would like a copy of the logo, drop me a line. LisaL.author@gmail.com. I'd be glad to share. I have both gold-foil and black-ink versions, or you can design your own.

Fated

Curse of the Hybrids
Book 7

LISA LAGALY

PUBLISHING

1

HONEY – NOVEMBER 30 – CANADA

Honey yawned and poked her head out from under the sagging bed to swivel her ears unimpeded. Someone was inside the house. She crept out of the sleeping bag and, shivering at the sudden loss of warmth, sent the bag to the nether with the tip of her tail. Being careful to avoid the creaky part of the floor, she padded to the top of the staircase and peeked down. Whoever it was hadn't made it to the steps yet. The beaded curtain she'd found elsewhere in the abandoned house and nailed up in the middle of the stairs was hanging quietly.

The musty scent of wolves wafted up the steps. Darn. She wouldn't be able to hide here anymore. Wait, she recognized that scent. A familiar furry head appeared at the bottom of the steps and looked right up at her. Tongue lolling, eyes wide with excitement, the wolf charged up the stairs and right through the beads, pulling the whole curtain down. He didn't even slow. A moment later he was all over Honey, yipping and licking and bouncing around her like a pup.

"Cede, you idiot. The floors aren't stable. You're going to bring the whole house down on top of us," a familiar voice yelled from the bottom of the stairs.

Honey transformed and pulled Cede into a hug, trying to get him to calm down. He did stop and rest his large head on his shoulder for a whole second before proceeding to swab the side of her face with his huge tongue.

She pushed him away with the dirtiest look she could conjure.

"Isabelle," Derrik called up the stairs, "can we come up?"

"You told them I was here?" Honey whispered.

Cede nodded excitedly.

"You know I'm in hiding, right?"

Cede gave her a wolfy grin.

"Are you here to kill or capture me?" Honey yelled down the stairs.

"Neither."

"What are you here for then?"

"Can't we visit as friends?"

"Am I a friend?"

"Unless you don't want to be." Derrik's head popped up above the level of the floor and he sniffed. "It really is you."

"Who did you expect?"

Rock's head popped up beside Derrik's. "Is it true you're part wolf?"

Honey transformed in response, earning a strong nuzzle from Cede. She popped back and trapped him in a headlock to give his head a vigorous rub.

"I knew no normal witch could run that fast," Derrik declared, finishing his climb to the top.

"Can you do that again?" Rock asked, gaping at her from the steps. Honey cocked her eyebrow at him, transformed with her eyebrow still cocked, then transformed again before turning to Derrik. "What are you guys doing here?"

"There were reports of a motorcycle and lights around this house. Alpha Aki sent us to check it out in case it was a rogue." He sniffed at her. "You're not a rogue are you?"

"I can't be a rogue. I'm a hybrid."

Cede whined and leaned against her.

"He says he wishes he were a hybrid," Derrik said, shaking his head.

"No, you don't. People tend to want to kill hybrids."

"Not us," Rock said, finally emerging from the stairs. He plopped down onto his knees so that he was facing her. "Have you always known you were a hybrid?"

"It's kind of hard not to know."

"You knew when you were here."

"Of course."

"But you weren't a Luna then?"

"No."

"You really are?" Derrik asked, squatting next to Cede and staring at her forehead. "Take off your hat."

She tugged off the beanie and waited patiently while he scanned her forehead.

"Those are real, eh?"

"I didn't draw them on."

Cede stepped back and started to transform.

"Don't do that," Derrik admonished. "Nobody wants to see your skinny naked ass."

"It's okay. I've got extra clothes." Honey flicked her wrist and pulled Jay's tent out of the nether complete with all the spare male clothes she had.

"Wow," Rock said while she dug out a pair of sweats and a hoodie. "Now I wish I was a hybrid. We could run wherever we wanted without worrying about carrying our clothes."

Honey held the clothes out to her side without looking behind her. A few seconds later, they vanished from her hand. Cede's transformation had gotten a lot faster.

"Who's your alpha?" Derrik asked.

"You wouldn't know him."

"That guy on TV said your alpha was dead," Cede said behind her.

"What guy?" She knew she should have gone back to the library yesterday. She'd felt so tired though after all the magic she'd expended breaking the curse and transporting people around, she'd gone to Canada and found a bed as soon as Vera and Michael had portalled back to Mr. Felix. A sense of exhilaration trickled through her as it donned on her that she'd not only saved three people, she'd scored another curse tablet. She only had one more piece of the curse to collect.

"The guy who called into WTV to verify you were a Luna."

"Who called in?"

"Someone from the Little pack in Indiana," Derrik responded.

She felt Cede move to her side.

"Did he say anything else?"

"Only that at your initiation ceremony you lit up brighter than the moon itself."

"Huh." Which one of her friends had called in and why? It was probably Nathan. He'd mentioned before the importance of making sure information was presented to the public with the right spin.

Cede touched her shoulder. "Did you love him?"

"Who?"

"Your alpha."

271

"Not romantically, no. He was nearly twice my age, but I did and do consider him a good friend."

"I was there when Alpha Aki chose our Luna. I was just a kid, but doesn't the Alpha have to be there when a Luna is presented to the moon?" Derrik asked.

"He was there – in spirit. I think I was the only one who could see him though."

What a horrible conversation to have right after she'd woken up and was shy a couple of meals. She dipped her head so the boys wouldn't see the tear crawling out of the corner of her eye. An arm pulled her to a chest that smelled like a combination of laundry detergent, Cede, and faintly of Jay.

"I'm sorry you lost your friend," Cede said. "I know what that's like."

He did. He truly did. She could smell his sincerity and sadness. That her funny go-lucky friend knew such loss made her even sadder and she gave up trying to contain her tears and let them pour out onto Cede's borrowed shirt.

"Geez Cede, you know just what to say, don't you," one of the guys said.

"It's not his fault," Honey sniffed, swiping her cheeks with her sleeve. "I'm hungry. I'll be much better after I eat."

She pulled her backpack out of the nether and started searching the pockets for a snack, keeping an eye on the three wolves at the same time. She trusted Cede not to tell anyone she was there. Rock and Derrik on the other hand, were decent guys but they were much more loyal to their alpha and therefore more likely to report her.

Derrik's phone dinged. He pulled it out and started

typing.

"You're not telling anyone I'm here are you?" Honey asked.

Derrik pressed one more button then held up his phone for Honey to see. She read:

Alpha Aki: Find anything?"

Me: A friend.

Another message popped up:

Alpha Aki: Isabelle?

Derrik typed *yes.*

Alpha Aki: Keep her there. I'm coming.

"Cede, can I have the clothes back? I better go." Where to though? Maybe the shed. Phooey, she was hoping for a good breakfast this morning.

Derrik typed something rapidly into his phone then held it up for Honey.

Me: We promised we wouldn't try to capture or kill her.

Alpha Aki: Tell her I just want to talk.

"Does he truly just want to talk or is he telling you that while planning to surround the house at the same time?"

"I don't know," Derrik admitted, frowning at his phone.

"Take me with you," Cede begged.

"I thought you liked your new pack."

"I'll like your pack better."

Honey leaned her forehead against his. "My pack is currently without an alpha. You need an alpha. Maybe someday, when this mess is behind me, you can join."

Cede threw his arms around her and squeezed her tight. "I love you."

"Jeez Cede, lay off." Rock leaned forward and pulled them apart. "Don't mind him. He tells girls he loves them

273

at least once a week."

"I do not."

"Isabelle." Derrik held up his phone again.

Me: She doesn't trust you.

Alpha Aki: She has my word, I only want to talk.

"What about the rest of the people with him?"

Derrik immediately typed in her response, then replied, "He says his beta just wants to listen."

All she remembered about Alpha Aki was that he was big and hairy and naked, but he had given Cede a chance after she'd pleaded his case. "I guess I can wait." She unwrapped the snack bar she'd uncovered and stuffed it into her mouth, then washed it down with all the water left in her water bottle. Her stomach gurgled angrily when she didn't immediately feed it something else.

Cede stood. "I'll be right back."

"Where are you going?"

"It's a surprise."

"A good one?" she asked.

He nodded and grinned, then disappeared down the stairs in Jay's sweats and pale bare feet.

"You better go with him," Derrik said to Rock.

"Where is he going?"

"Who knows with him," Derrik replied.

Rock disappeared down the stairs too.

Honey pulled out another bar. She felt a little better but now her mouth was dry.

Downstairs, the front door creaked and wood popped, announcing Alpha Aki's arrival. That was fast. He must not have been very far away. Honey sent her tent and her pack into the nether and made sure there was nothing else laying around in case she needed to make a quick exit.

"I'm coming up."

Honey scooted closer to the stairs. There were only two people that she could see, but she froze them and Derrik, then took a quick look out of the window behind the house. She didn't see anyone or any vehicles. She slipped past Alpha Aki on the stairs and peered around Alpha Aki's beta to make sure no one else was in the room below. Only one vehicle was parked in the front and she couldn't smell anyone else. Perhaps Alpha Aki truly meant her no harm. She still searched him and his beta's pockets on her way back up the stairs. The beta had a gun which she emptied of bullets, and a taser from which she removed the batteries. Alpha Aki only had a phone which she was tempted to search to see if he'd told anyone where she was, but she'd already refroze him once. She put the phone back and ran back up the stairs to sit by Derrik before she unfroze them all.

"Where are Cede and Rock?" their alpha asked as soon as he reached the top the stairs and took a look around.

"Cede ran off like he does so I sent Rock after him."

Alpha Aki's eyes fell on her face, then flicked up to her still uncovered forehead. "Luna."

"Alpha."

"Where is the alpha who claims you?"

"I do not need an alpha's protection."

"Did you kill him?"

"No."

Alpha Aki wrinkled his nose. "I smell guilt."

"It was due to a mistake on my part that he died. I should have sent him home before trying to break the curse."

She forced back the tears and kept her head up so she

275

could keep an eye on the two men in front of her. The beta was trying to slip unnoticed past the alpha to stand out of her sight.

"Mr. Beta, stay where you are so I can keep an eye on you please."

Alpha Aki nodded and the beta stopped, but Honey noted how the beta positioned his hand over the pocket with the gun.

"What did you want to speak to me about?"

"Will you show me your wolf?"

She knew why but she still asked, "Why?"

"Do you know what you are?"

"I do, but you must not since you're asking me to make myself vulnerable to you and your beta."

He dropped down to the floor so that his knees were folded underneath him and motioned to his beta to do the same. "Please. I have to be sure before I do this."

"Do what?"

"Pledge myself and my pack to you."

The beta's eyes didn't move from her, but his frown was clear enough. He didn't like the idea.

"Why would you do that? You're an alpha. You're basically a king."

"A Celestial Luna is higher than the alphas. Think of it like an empress or perhaps a queen above lords. As to why – the moon favors those who submit to her chosen, plus if I make a formal pledge to you as a luna I am not legally required to kill you or turn you in. You can stay with my pack as long as you need and we will protect you."

The beta's frown shifted from her to his alpha.

"That's extremely generous, although I wouldn't ask that of anyone. What do you get out of it?"

"Besides an alliance with a person who can cure rogues and break spells?"

"Yes."

"Isn't that enough?"

"That's all you want of me?"

"All?" He gave a halfhearted chuckle. "Do you know how many rogues I've had to put down in my life because there was no way to heal them? I feel like I lose a little of my soul every time. I've got two I'm holding right now that should have already been put down, but I was hoping I'd run across you again."

He hadn't quite answered her question, but what he had said sounded sincere.

"Would you expect me to join your pack?"

"No. Like I said, you're above alphas, although if you did want to join my pack I would welcome you."

The beta wrinkled his nose behind Alpha Aki's back.

"You and Cede would probably be the only ones."

Alpha Aki snorted.

Derrik elbowed her. "Hey, I wouldn't mind. Show him your wolf."

Alpha Aki started to rise. "I can g... Fudge!"

Honey winked at him in her wolf form, then transformed back into her human one.

"Fudge?" she asked.

"Luna Leia doesn't like it when he cusses. She makes him sleep in an actual doghouse," Derrik whispered loudly.

"I think I like your luna already."

Alpha Aki didn't even crack a smile. Instead he bowed over his knees until his head was on the dusty floor. "Great Luna before me, I pledge myself and my pack into your service. Our teeth are your teeth. Our claws are your claws. Our fires are your fires and our food is your food. Please accept our humble offering and deign to place your protection over my pack."

"Um..wow. There's probably something official I'm supposed to say to that but…"

The itch in her thumb that had started during Alpha Aki's speech was now starting to feel painful and hot. She lifted her hand to knock away whatever was biting her and was shocked to find her thumb lit up like a glow-stick. It felt like hands were guiding her when she reached down to lift Alpha Aki's great head far enough to place her glowing thumb in the center of his forehead.

"I accept your pledge. Receive the gift you most desire."

Even though she wasn't the one directing the molecules into the right places, she understood what was happening. The many connections in Alpha Aki's mind were strengthened and realigned to withstand the harshest of attacks. As a last touch, she added an anchor to a minuscule section of her thumb.

"There. I have…"

Something heavy hit her in the side, sending her crashing through the wooden railing around the stairs. She was so used to sending herself to the nether, that she did it on reflex while still in midair. A moment later, she popped back into the storage space in the unfinished part of the second floor where she'd placed her latest anchor. Through the thin walls, it wasn't hard at all to hear Alpha Aki yelling.

"What did you do?!"

From the limited view she had between the slats in the

wall, it looked like he was yelling down the stairs.

"My job. I was protecting you!" A male voice yelled up the stairs.

"From a little girl with a glowing thumb? Gee thanks."

"She had you under her thumb for ten minutes at least. What did she do to you?"

Alpha Aki shook his head slowly. "I'm not sure. I don't feel any different."

"I strengthened your mind so you don't have to worry about accepting rogues into your pack and I made it so you can talk to me," Honey sent telepathically. *"Nod if you can hear me."*

Alpha Aki nodded and looked around. Her thumbprint shone brightly in the center of his forehead.

"It also looks like I marked you. That might fade though."

"Great Luna, please accept my apology for my beta's actions."

"She came back?" the voice called. "Derrik, protect the alpha!"

"I'm fine Derrik. Go downstairs and see if he broke anything."

Downstairs, the door creaked open again. She heard a faint "What happened?" before the mouth-watering scent of sausage and hash browns filtered up the steps and directly to her hiding place. Her stomach let out an embarrassing roar that had everyone turning her way.

"Hang on, I'm coming!" Cede called from below.

"Don't you dare go past me, you two-bit fleabag."

"Piers, let him pass."

"Alpha, you've been compromised. Let me handle this."

"I said, let him pass."

Honey didn't bow under the command, but she could

tell from the way Alpha Aki swelled and the way Derrik flinched, that it was a strong one.

"And put your phone away. I made a pledge. She is under our protection. Anyone who attempts to harm or turn her in will be immediately ousted from the pack!" Alpha Aki called down the stairs before turning to her wall. "You can come out now. I promise none of us here will harm you."

Like there was any way she would say no to hash browns.